A
LAGOS
LOVE
STORY

A LAGOS LOVE STORY

Zainab Kabir

WORDS
RHYMES &
RHYTHM

Printed and Published in Nigeria by:
Words Rhymes & Rhythm Limited
Suite C309, Global Plaza Plot 366, Obafemi
Awolowo Way, Jabi District, Abuja, Nigeria.
08169027757, 08060109295
www.wrr.ng

DEDICATION

A Lagos Love story is Dedicated to my parents, Mr and Mrs Kabir Talata, and to all other beautiful souls out there.

ACKNOWLEDGEMENT

Many thanks to my tireless readers, who have read and supported my work from the very beginning when I was still very unsure of myself. Thank you to my wattpad friends who kept inspiring me, I can't mention names but I appreciate all.

Thank you to my family, without whom I wouldn't have been able to withstand the harshness of the writer's world. I couldn't have asked for any better.

Many thanks to my wonderful, extremely supportive friends, Hanifah, Fadilah, Nabilah, Hafsat, Aisha, Kamal, Victor and to my other friends. Special thanks to my most honest and supportive critic, El-abari.

Many thanks to the organisers of the Green Authors Prize and the words rhymes and rhythm publishers. Thank you for everything.

My Greatest appreciation goes to God Almighty.

PROLOGUE

I've always thought of life as a book, with everyone having his or her own story, and that we were all characters in each other's books.

Sometimes people come into our lives to make up our stories, some people make up chapters, others just pages and paragraphs, either ways they all form part of your story.

I'm about to tell you a story, I'm not starting from the beginning nor is it the end, just where my plot completely changed.

Two shots of bullets came breaking through the glass window, shattering it to a million pieces. Eyes brave enough turned in direction of the sudden intrusion while mine shut instantly and trembled, like my entire body.

"Get down!" one of dad's bodyguards yelled, and within seconds Dad and I were beneath the table with his bodyguards somehow magically surrounding us. With my heart beating way too fast and warm tears freely rolling down my eyes, I held my breath and tried to pray to God, I mumbled some words which I was sure were not English, but I knew God would understand the language of fear.

It was way beyond what I was used to. I had gotten letters full of threats, but usually they just messed with each other in their own ways. But gunshots, that was just too far. My father was part of the lawyers in the prosecuting team of a case of treason, and he had been threatened with several warnings to withdraw from the case like the rest of his colleagues had, but unfortunately my father had always been a stubborn man, who never would quit on anything he had started. I loved my father and admired his personality, but all it had ever led to was trouble for him and us, and I could no longer keep track of the number of times I had wished he was a little bit different, a little bit less. Of course these wishes were always followed by guilt.

We waited until it felt safe enough, but even then, my heart wouldn't stop thumping. "Calm down sweetie. Are you okay?" my father asked after about five minutes of hiding under the table, silently, that is if the sound of my beating heart and father's heavy breathing were excluded. His dark eyes had become darker, and the wrinkled lines on his fore head, folded in worry. I had always acted strong in front of my father; I always thought he needed someone as strong as he was by his side.

"No, but I will be," I let out a sigh and started crawling out of the table when I heard the glass shatter again, making me crawl back immediately. This time it wasn't a gunshot but a brown parcel.

A short, chubby body guard whose name I couldn't remember clearly, despite his size, swiftly moved to the parcel, picked it up and brought it closer to his ears. He was about to open it when a tall bearded bodyguard, whose name I didn't know stopped him with his hand.

"Careful" he eyed the parcel before turning to look at us. "Sir, miss, please stay down," Dad nodded and I buried my head in between my knees shielding it with my hands. Honestly, at that moment I was ready to be blown up, yet strangely I couldn't help but think of how interesting the whole episode would have been if it was in a movie.

The tall body guard collected the parcel from the short one and gently placed it on the floor before he quickly opened it and then they both ran to take cover. I waited for it to explode but it didn't. I think we all knew that it wouldn't.

When it was clear that it wasn't going to explode, the tall body guard picked up the parcel which contained a small yellow note.

"What's on it?" Dad asked firmly and unshaken. The short bodyguard collected the note and read out in a shaky voice, "Stop now or you would be responsible for whatever happens to your family."

***

By family they meant me, I was the only family my Father had in America- only remaining family. My mother had died a year ago during my graduation in a car accident, and I was an only child.

My parents were Nigerians by birth but I was born in America, so I considered myself a complete American since I had never even smelt the shores of Nigeria. Once upon a time we were a happy and complete African American family, while my father was an environmental lawyer and my mother, a paediatrician. We were happy, I liked to believe, until my father decided environmental law wasn't what he was born for and started pursuing more daring things. That night on the dining table, when he told my mother and I, I was so proud of him, but I guess if I knew it was going to be the beginning of our doom, I may have stopped him. He wouldn't have listened, and we would have had a huge fight which would have lasted days, until I gave in.

We didn't sleep at our house that night because it wasn't safe for some reasons triggered by my dad's defiance as regards a pending court case. So we packed some stuffs and left to stay at a hotel. All I wanted to do was find a bed, lay my head and sleep away my entire problems, but I doubted I would be able to do that. I had learnt from my short time alive, that sleep was like alcohol, it makes you forget for a while, until you're sober again. In the end you can't sleep forever or drink forever. You could, but it's called death in the end.

"Are you okay dear?" Dad asked as we settled down in the hotel room. He looked like he had aged ten more years in just a few hours. I took in a deep breath as I sank on the king sized bed, rested my head on the pillow, and stared at the golden chandelier hanging from the beige coloured ceiling.

"I'm fine," I lied.

He frowned and moved to sit next to me. I tore my gaze away from the chandelier, and turned to look at him as his big palms covered mine, one slightly resting on my palm, and the other drawing invisible circles below.

"I am so sorry Hilal, I'll fix everything. You don't have to worry; I'll do everything to make sure you're okay," he paused and inhaled deeply as if it pained him to breath, " I'll never let anything happen to you." His eyes bore into mine and I knew that he meant every word. I felt safe.

I squeezed his hands slightly and said "You have to be okay too dad, you're all I have and I need you"

"I need you too" he kissed my hands, before his phone rang, "goodnight cupcake," he whispered as he picked up the call and left the room in long strides.

"Goodnight soldier," I whispered back. I didn't know what to expect but I hoped everything would be okay by the time I opened my eyes the next day. So I closed my eyes and waited for sleep to take over. It took a while, but I finally fell into a dreamless sleep.

I was woken up by someone shaking me, at first I thought I was dreaming, but with the persistent shaking, it became obvious that it wasn't a dream.

"Miss, wake up," I heard a familiar voice saying over and over again.

"What...." I asked groggily, still slumbering.

"Wake up else you're going to miss your flight," said the familiar voice. Flight? That woke me up. I quickly sat up pushing the blankets away from my body.

"What flight?" I asked, looking weary but wide eyed.

It was Jason, the driver. He stood straighter and put his hands behind him, bodyguard style. "You're leaving to Nigeria by 4:00am, if you don't hurry; you're going to be late miss." I had known Jason for five years, and he had always been formal, but never had I seen him look so serious, or worried.

I was confused; I laughed "Jason, you're joking, right?" I looked at him desperate for an answer; I knew he wasn't joking, since he wasn't the type to even laugh at a joke. He looked uncomfortable, he kept fidgeting. He coughed and replied "No miss, I am not."

"Where is dad?" I asked as I put my feet on the floor, searching for my flip flops with my legs.

"He left already, uhm... he didn't want to wake you up, but he left this for you," he gave me a long brown envelope. It had my father's stamps all over it, as if he wanted me to know it was truly from him. "There's no time. We have to go now."

I was pensive, shocked and still a little bit sleepy but I decided to obey, I didn't have a list of choices. I picked up my bag which was still lying on the floor where I had thrown it before falling asleep, and followed Jason to the car. Some of my belongings from home had already been put it the trunk. I was sure I slept for only three hours, and that my father had spent those three hours developing a plan, if I could call it that.

As we drove to the airport, I picked up the envelope and slipped out a white paper which had my father's cursive and slightly slanted handwriting on it and it read;

Dear Hilal,

I'm sorry. I don't know if you know how sorry I am, and I don't think I could ever tell you how much, even if I lived a hundred years more.

What I can do, is to protect you with everything I have. Maybe I'm just being paranoid but I feel that what happened last night was just a tip off the ice berg, and I know these people would go to any length. For your safety, I know I should leave the case, but then again I know you'd want me to do the right thing, and the right thing to do in this case would be to stay and fight for what's right.

Hilal, you are my only weakness, you're everything I've got, and knowing this, they'll do everything to get to you because they know that's the only way to get to me. I found out that there had been someone stalking you for the past month, and I know that if you stay, it would only get worse.

I want you to leave to Nigeria, for a couple of months, just until things sizzle down. There is no assurance that sending you to Nigeria would mean your safety, which is why you're going to have to lay really low.

All my accounts have been frozen, I don't have much, so I can't promise a very comfortable life in Nigeria, you are going to have to blend a whole lot, but it will only be until I can unfreeze my accounts.

Imran would be there to help you with whatever you need. Everything you need to travel, your passport, your driver's license, Nigerian national identity card, cash, etc. They are all in the envelope.

Finally, I need a bigger favour from you; I need you to take care of yourself and try to stay safe. Don't worry about me; I'll be fine as long as you are. I love you.

Love, Dad.

I read the letter again for the third time, struggling to stifle the tears that threatened to break through. But I couldn't, my eyes were way too lubricated by the emotions triggered by the letter's content.

I shouldn't have been crying, I should have been stronger, like my father always said I was. Right? But I felt weak and couldn't do anything but surrender to that moment of vincibility.

Jason watched me through the rear-view mirror as I cried, and I knew he felt pity for me. Although he didn't say anything, the expression on his face betrayed his feelings.

I managed to pull myself together as we closed in on the airport. As we approached it, I searched through the contents of the envelope, picked what was supposed to be my passport and opened it. There was an old picture of me on it, one which I hated but my father especially liked. He said it reminded him of my mother when he first met her. It barely looked like me. I smiled at the memory, but my smile almost immediately vanished when I saw the name on the passport, it wasn't Hilal Sadiq, but Hadizat Farouq. I searched though the other documents and it was all the same, Hadizat Farouq plastered on all of them.

A little *"p.s, you also get a change of identity"* would have been great. It was the smart thing to do though, if those people were as bad as my father said they were, then it would be very easy for them to find me If I used my name. I repeated the name 'Hadizat' several times, until it flowed freely and normally from my lips.

As soon as I stood in front of the airport, I made a promise to myself, to pretend that nothing that happened really happened and that I wasn't really who I was. I was Hadizat Farouq, a normal Fully Nigerian graduate. Brave, ambitious, and free spirited.

CHAPTER ONE

HADIZAT

The flight was going to be fourteen long hours. It would have been great if my father had at least put a book in that envelope of his, but that would have been the last thing on his mind following his efforts in trying to protect my life and his. I had the phone my father had put in the envelope, but it was the type that had no internet, it just made calls. I hadn't seen such a phone since the time my Grandmother visited from Nigeria. She swore it was better and smarter than all our smart phones combined. As much as I tried to convince her to move on from the 90's, it didn't work at all.

I thought the journey was going to be super boring but just then I looked to my left and an actor, model, or maybe a perfect sculpture was sitting right next to me. I was simply awed. There was no way he could be human, and if he was, he definitely wasn't ordinary. He was moving and reading a book, so he passed the human check list. I didn't need a genius to tell me that he wasn't ordinary though.

Yes I was still the same, same girl who was almost killed a few hours ago, same girl who was now acting like a crazy fan girl, who just met her idol. Technically though, I wasn't the same. I was a very good liar, but I couldn't lie to myself enough to completely fall into the lie.

Maybe my flight wouldn't be so boring, I thought to myself, as I turned to gawk at my seatmate. I tried starting a conversation with him.

"Hi," I said, and then I thought about what to say for a second. "My name's Hadizat Farouq. It's my first time going to Nigeria. Are you Nigerian?" I wasn't even surprised at how freely the lie flowed from my mouth.

For the first time since the flight started he turned and looked at me through his reading glasses for a second or two, then without a word he put his hand into his breast pocket and slipped out a card and gave it to me and then he continued reading his book. Strange? Yes I thought it was, but I didn't ponder much on it, instead I pondered on how captivating his eyes were, how straight his nose was, as if God had stopped to use a ruler for it, his jawline, and... I didn't let myself complete the thought, I was moving too close to sin.

I looked at the complimentary card he had given me, his name was Salim Abubakar. He worked at a construction company called galaxy in Nigeria, Lagos precisely. For some reason I was really excited, my heart was racing faster than normal. I turned again to access him properly; indeed he was stunning, looks, like that of a mannequin, perfect in every physical aspect. How he was not a model or an actor was what I found most surprising.

"Are you planning on boring a hole into my face with that stare of yours?" he asked, still not looking at my face. His voice was husky, but velvety smooth and he had a Nigerian accent. He had caught me staring, and usually I would have felt embarrassed, but at that moment I wasn't the least bit embarrassed, but maybe it had to do with the fact that my brain wasn't really functioning properly at that moment.

"Sorry," I grinned and looked away. If the normally rational me would see what I had just done, she'd be shaking her head and giving me a disappointed look, but the new me took chances and made bold, embarrassing, and life altering moves. After that conversation which wasn't really a conversation, to be honest, we both said nothing until I fell asleep.

I woke up hours later and saw Salim asleep. His eyelashes were so long they rested below his eyes, and his eye brows furrowed together, almost forming a uni-brow. His chest bounced slowly and gently in rhythm with the sound of his breathing. I watched him sleep for a long time before falling asleep again, and just for that moment, I completely forgot my problems.

I was woken up by the voice of pilot announcing our arrival. I started to unbuckle the seatbelts but before I could do that, Salim had already walked away without saying a word to me. Of course, nothing would ever really be perfect, he may have looked like he fell right out of heaven, but his personality was seriously lacking. I couldn't care less though; I was never going to see him again anyway.

The airport was the noisiest, craziest, and busiest place I had ever seen. There were so many people moving around as if in circles, I could swear there were fights going on in every corner, passengers with guards, passengers with other passengers, yelling and cursing in different languages. To make it worse, the AC's in the airport were completely useless, some weren't working and others blowing hot air. I was hot, tired, frustrated, and had nowhere to seat because all the seats were occupied. It took forever to find my luggage, through the very disorganised and distinct smelling crowd. Clearing customs was no walk in the park either; thankfully all my papers were complete and valid, thanks to my Father. The officers were rude and one of them kept staring at my behind, and touching me unnecessarily, and even when I eyed him, he just winked and flashed his yellow knocked out teeth. The girl behind me wouldn't tolerate it though, as she insulted the life out of the officer, while he just kept on calling her áshawo. Leaving the airport in one piece felt like my greatest achievement, but I would come to realize that surviving in Lagos, would be an even greater achievement.

I found a taxi driver who was ready to take me all the way to Victoria Island, and introduce me to Lagos, at double the price. He was a middle aged fair man, with a moustache and a cartoonish smile. He had the most trustworthy face I saw amongst the other drivers, and I was always a good judge of character. He asked me to call him Baba Lucky. His cab looked old, but not knocked up.

He looked confused when I spoke at first, so I had to fix my accent and it wasn't too hard because I had a lot of African friends when I was in high school and my college best friend and roommate, Shade, was a Nigerian. There was a time I was fascinated with the accent only because my Nigerian parents lacked an accent, so while other normal people were busy learning British and Australian accents, I was learning a Nigerian accent and Yoruba language. I may have succeeded in learning the accent, but honestly, I failed miserably in learning the Yoruba language, only because Shade gave up on me too soon.

He smiled and muttered something in Yoruba language. "Oya anty enter," he said, carrying my luggage into the trunk of his vehicle. For a moment I wondered why he was calling me anty, it was obvious he was way older than I was, but as I settled down in the car, I started thinking about how I was going to survive in this strange country. I could say that I had been living an umbrella, always protected and guarded. As an only child, I enjoyed the privileges to the fullest. My parents were always over protective and I never could complain of lacking their attention, despite their busy jobs. What was I to do with no one but Imran, which equalled no one. Imran was the real free spirit; he lived life like he was going to die tomorrow. It was always a roller coaster with no stops, and lots of crashing and rising. He had come for his Grandmother's funeral from America, five years ago, and never returned. He said living felt more like living in Nigeria. I never understood what that meant. Soon I would come to understand what he meant.

Imran had asked me to meet him at yellows shop, Bar beach, victoria island. I was supposed to call him before leaving the airport, but when I checked my back for my phone, it was nowhere to be found. I thought it fell off, but Baba Lucky swore it was stolen, I believed him.

I didn't have a phone to call him, so I prayed he would wait for me there. I had no idea how hard it was going to be getting there, no idea.

CHAPTER TWO

SALIM

As soon as the plane landed, I tried to get out not just because I was late for the company's dinner, but also because I was scared of that woman's beauty. She was very beautiful and looked like she had been sent down by the devil himself. I tried to put on my coldest act but I still felt my heart beating way too fast, maybe it was because of the way she was staring at me and maybe it was something more.

My father always said women were poisonous snakes, covered in very fine skin. They come into your life, make you feel good, rip you off of your heart, money and then leave you shattered and a little broke. I always believed him.

My mother, being the number one reason for his distrust in women, and also his theory about love being nothing more than a foolish fabrication of romance novels, movies and fairy tales being instilled in human minds from the beginning of time. It had been twenty two years and I still saw the hurt in his eyes whenever he spoke of her. As for me, I never used to think of her. She didn't exist to me.

"Take me to galaxy," I said to the driver as I got into the car. I sat quietly at the back seat and the name 'Hadizat Farouq' kept ringing in my head over and over again. I was perplexed because I had better things to think about but instead I kept thinking of her. Thinking of her felt useless and worthless, for all I knew I might never see her again. One thing I was sure of was that she was going to call me, all the women I had ever given my complimentary card to, never hesitate in calling me, and she'd be no different.

I got to the party quite late. All the guests were already there, looking like they always did, dressed in over prized suits and dresses, and the party elegant as always, with the finest wines, food and service. As soon as I entered the room, I ransacked the place with my eyes, for the most important person in my life, the strongest and most inspiring man I knew, my father.

"You're here," I heard him say from behind me. I turned and in front of me stood a very tall, well-built man, in a very well-tailored suit. With a nose resembling mine and eyes as clear as the morning, he didn't look a day over forty.

"Ina wuni Baba (Good evening\afternoon)" I greeted him with an automatic smile on my face.

"Lafiya kalau. How was your flight? I've been waiting for you. Zo (Come), there's someone I want you to meet," he said excitedly leading me forward. My father had a very unique way of showing affection, I had been away for two months, and his "I miss you" was same as his "I've been waiting for you", I understood him, because I wasn't any better than he was. I followed him wondering why he was so excited.

"Salim, this is Fatima Aliyu," he introduced me to a way too fair, way too skinny woman who wore a black long dress and a navy blue veil. She had a confident look on her face, the kind you would see on the face of a super model. She was tall too and to compliment her looks, she had the fakest smile anyone could ever wear.

"Fatima, this is my son Salim," her gaze was eye piercing and almost intimidating. Almost.

"*Salam alaikum*, how do you do Salim?" she asked, now grinning.

"*Wa alaikum as salam*, I'm good and I know you are too, it shows." She blushed and then laughed. I wasn't really a flirt, but I knew just the cheesiest lines to use on women like her, and I was quite the expert in complimenting women who needed compliments to breathe.

"I'll leave you two now to get to know each other," my father winked at me and I raised a brow in disapproval before he disappeared into the crowd with a mischievous grin on his face. I wasn't sure exactly what his motives were but I was going to play along, like I always did.

I walked with Fatima to the balcony, where we sat down 'to get to know each other.'

"So tell me about yourself" I said as we sat on the bench on the balcony. She blushed as she took a sip from her wine and sat on the bench.

"Well, I don't like to talk about myself, but since you asked, I'm the first daughter of Aliyu Isa Asabe of Marvel team limited."

The moment she said whose daughter she was I understood it all. My Father had been hoping to partner with Marvel team for years, and now that he had this opportunity, I was positive he wouldn't let it go. He didn't care much for women, but good business deals, oh he loved them. Strangely, I wasn't the slightest bit hurt that my father was using me to get what he wanted. I'd do the same with him, if the tables were turned.

The rest of the night passed by as Fatima kept yammering on and on about herself. Lord, it was frustrating. It was like she was reading a really long pre written speech about her. For a person who didn't like talking about herself, she had a lot to say. It was my fault for asking, and I regretted it, but realised something that night; I really didn't like her but it didn't matter, it was just business after all.

HADIZAT

As Baba lucky drove through the streets of Lagos, I confirmed I had just arrived on another planet. Lagos was no New Zealand, nor New York, it was a whole different kind of new. There were no skyscrapers, or high city lights and romantic music playing in the back ground, but they were a handful of tall buildings surrounded by shacks, and houses with rusty roofs and sheets, scattered with barely any spacing from afar. The streets were barely paved and others needed renovation, exploding gutters, which were also used as waste dumps, and broken street lights. Stalls in every corner painted the colour of dirt, with writings like "Olamide for life," "Akin AKA brave soul was here," "ice block for sail," and big red "x" marks which showed approval or remove. There wasn't much electricity in the city, except for the tall buildings that were very bright, the rest of the city looked dim with orange lights, lamps and candles.

The music playing at the background of Lagos was a mix of afro beat, Rnb, old Westlife songs, the sound of hundreds of tiny generators, honks, bleats, and roars from arguments. Together they created a sound of chaos, a type of chaos that seemed built with the city.

While places like Paris and New York smelled like romance, Lagos was made up of a cacophony of the smell of gutters, oil, spicy foods, meat, sweat, petrol, smoke, hot air and dust. You could literally taste the smell at the back of your throat, the smell was overwhelming and actually nice, when the car was moving, but other times when we were stuck in traffic jams, or congestion as Baba lucky had called it, the smell was intolerable and I had to battle with myself whether I wanted to smell the fumes that poured from the engines of uncountable mini buses, motor bikes and tricycles, or smell Baba Lucky's car that smelt like dead rats and rotten food.

Ultimately, I was forced to smell Baba Lucky's car that by the way didn't have an AC, because the roads were too risky with hawkers pushing all sort of things through the window. One time when my eyes met with a short middle aged man selling panties and Bra's, he immediately shoved them through the window and asked me to try a bra on. That was how slow traffic was, the hawkers would have time to move around and come back to meet you in the same spot. Baba Lucky seemed to love complaining about Lagos. He loved Lagos and its chaos, and would have nothing to talk about if Lagos wasn't as chaotic as it was. He would occasionally wind down the glass of his window and rain abuses on the drivers of the mini buses, which he called Danfos and

Molues, then wind up again and talk about how reckless drivers in Lagos were.

After a while when the drivers got frustrated, some started honking continuously, and Baba lucky joined them, shouting "fly now" and spitting some words in Yoruba, soon the driver of a yellow cab came out of his car and went and grabbed the collar of a Toyota Camry driver, accusing him of scratching the back of his knocked up cab. As if on queue, other drivers had come out of their cars, and were trying to stop a fist fight between the Toyota driver and the taxi driver. If the "congestion" hadn't chosen that time to move, I was sure Baba Lucky would have joined them. I was thankful we were finally moving.

We passed a neighbourhood that smelled like fresh grass and fresh water, with paved roads and bright houses into a neighbourhood that Baba lucky called Ojuelegba, also known as The Devils Den or The Cursed Land, and insisted that all windows be closed. He narrated how he was robbed in the morning in front of the police once, and another incident when he was beaten black and blue for not having a ticket or money for ticket to pass through a particular street. I got chills when I saw what he was talking about, the streets were dim and busy, ugly and congested, cars moved very slowly as the roads were very bad, and touts lurked in every corner and the police looked like they were best friends with the touts. As if the curse was following Baba lucky, the car developed problems right in the middle of the streets of ojuelegba and he had to park and pour water on the engine. It took less than two minutes with Baba lucky hurrying like it was the end of the world, but when he entered the car, a dark policeman wearing all black clothes and shades with a baseball bat entered with him, and asked him to drive to the police station for parking wrongly. Baba lucky didn't even try to explain, he simply apologized and brought out a two hundred naira note and squeezed into the policeman's hand. The policeman quickly alighted the car, promising to deal with him next time. I had just witnessed bribery and corruption, and I had no questions to ask, I was still taking Lagos in. I would soon come to realize that that was how things were settled in Lagos.

It was about 9:00 nine pm when I got to Bar beach, tired and moments away from breaking down. The entrance to the beach was rowdy, with traders selling everything from food to clothes, one trader was even selling shades. Some women were selling corn, bean balls, fried yam and many other fried foods that I recognised only because of Shade who took me to African restaurants sometimes and the other ones I was going to find out about soon.

Some men on another side were grilling fish and meat. Some other men were arguing at a corner, while others were drinking and smoking. Most of the children were gathered in a circle playing on the sand.

There were prostitutes in skimpy clothing and heavy make-up, doing well what prostitutes would. There was a long queue to the beach with a bunch of boys dressed like they were in a 90's hip hop music video, collecting money from the people on the beach. One had to pay money to get into a beach in Lagos, I marvelled. I decided to ask for yellows shop before entering the beach, and no one would know the beach better than traders, I thought.

"Good evening," I greeted the big, dark, kind faced woman selling roasted bananas.

"Which one you want?" she pointed at some of the bananas on the grill, "make I put pepper well well."

I nodded because I wasn't sure what exactly she was asking but I knew she wanted me to buy bananas, "yes. Ok but only one" I blurted. She picked up one hot banana with her bare hands, cut and poured grinded pepper with palm oil on it, and then she wrapped it with a newspaper before putting them into a black nylon bag. I grabbed a five hundred naira note from my envelope and asked her to keep the change. She studied me like I was strange for a few seconds before smiling and thanking me repeatedly.

"Where can I find yellows shop? Is it close?"

She looked at me but didn't answer, instead she yelled out a name "Kenny" and a girl came running to her.

Kenny was a tall, caramel skinned girl with small face. She wore a sleeveless top and a wrapper. She had very long braids that were almost reaching her waist. The woman told Kenny something in Yoruba language. The girl smiled and greeted me.

"Anty good evening, how may I help you. My mum doesn't understand English well," she said maintaining her big, pretty smile.

I couldn't understand how I had suddenly become everyone's aunty but I pushed the thought to the back of my mind, maybe it was a Nigerian thing.

"Hi, my name is Hil...Hadizat," I extended my hand forward for a handshake. "Can you direct me to yellows shop please?"

"You must be a visitor, everyone here knows yellow. Come with me, I'll show you." She took my hands and pulled me lightly past the bunch of Jay z wanna be's.

"We didn't pay," I started wondering what the reason was for such special treatment.

"Pay keh?" she laughed almost hysterically, "those fools are just my idiot neighbour and his friends. They think they own the beach, but they know who their mate is," she spoke like she was ready to fight, and I just thought of how she still hadn't let go of my hand.

Inside the beach there was a party going on, men and women drinking , dancing and pouring alcohol on each other, it looked like the kind of party you would wake up and find yourself buried in sand with a terrible hangover. We passed them to a place with lots of purple tents.

She took me to the only yellow tent there, it was large and crowded, mostly with men, but a few women were there too, sitting on yellow plastic chairs, drinking beer and chatting, while watching soccer on a big black screen

"We are here," she grinned. 'I'll leave you here now Deeza, bye". She called me Deeza, and I thought it was cute.

"Ok, Kenny. Thank you so much for your help. I hope to meet you again," she hugged me briefly and waved goodbye. She was the most comfortable person I had ever met, considering the fact that I wasn't much of a people person.

I looked around the place for Imran but I couldn't see him, then I heard someone whistle behind me. I turned around and I saw Imran. Tall, dark and good looking. Big eyes, slender nose and pearly white teeth. Nothing had changed about him, except the new low cut, it looked better on him than the old afro did. He wore a navy blue v neck shirt that hugged his body and dark jeans.

"Hey, hey, hey short woman," he smiled with his arms open wide.

I was so excited to see him; I didn't know how much I had missed him until I saw him again. I walked slowly towards him before jumping into his arms like a wild woman. I hugged him tight, oblivious to the sudden attention we were getting from the people around. He hugged me back for a few seconds before pushing me away slightly.

"Hey you want to ruin my reps?" I laughed; he was still the same cocky and funny man I knew.

"Nice meeting location," I said sarcastically.

"Well you know me, I always go for the best," he smirked, wiping away non-existent dust from his shirt.

"Why didn't you come to pick me, do you know what I've been through today?" I hit his shoulder slightly, "I don't even have a phone now."

"I couldn't risk being seen at that airport, besides Lagos was dying to introduce itself to you."

"Trust me, no one would have seen you at that airport," I said reminiscing on my horrible experience. "I'm hungry."

He took me to a fancy tent called "The Shrine" where I was served rice and a soup with assorted sea food. There were shrimps, prawns, cat fish and what not, while he ate the bananas I had bought earlier with soda. As I ate hungrily, Imran teased me just like he always did whenever he caught me eating meat, because when we were in college, I had pretended to be a vegetarian to impress my sorority sisters. After three months of not being able to eat meat, I gave up when I realized that I loved meat more than I loved a bunch of strangers I called my sisters.

We chatted for a long time, before he decided to take me to my new home. He didn't bring his car because he had just washed it and couldn't risk driving through the streets of Obalende, where he was taking me.

"We'll take an Okada," he informed me, when we were finally outside the beach.

"What's that?"

He pointed at a motorbike and I was sure he saw the fear that was flashing through my face, and if he didn't, then he must have heard it from my voice when I told him I didn't want to die.

"Relax, it's totally safe. At least most times, and you can finally cross it off your bucket list. It was on your journal." I wasn't even surprised because I always suspected that he was reading my journal in college.

We drove through the streets of Lagos, with my luggage in front of the driver and with me clutching his jacket like I was going to rip it off, the fresh smell of water, meat, and the cold dry air stood out amongst the smell of gutters, and grappled through my clothes and veil. I lost myself for a moment in the sound and smell of Lagos and I was able to not think about falling. I wanted the ride to never stop, but it did when we reached Obalende. A place that seemed alive and in sync, like everything was a piece of art. Forget the rowdiness, and congestion, the life and splendour was over powering, the colours were beautiful, and the chattering of people calmed my soul. Maybe it was the food, the bike ride or just my Americana genes setting in, but I saw Lagos in a different light, the beauty in chaos, and the serenity in the cacophony of distinct voices and loud music.

We stopped at a street called Keffi Street and then we entered a building. The gate to the building was broken, and the cemented floor was wet. It was a complex with similar looking apartments, ten all together. Each facing one another. Some rooms had buckets in front of them, others benches and two or three of them were decorated with flower pots with wilted flowers. It was quiet and looked like no one was around.

"Here's your room," we stopped at the last room in the complex. I stared at the front of the apartment, not exactly what I was feeling. "Look, it might not look like it's the best but it really is; It's the safest", he said holding my shoulder.

I sighed and groaned, "it doesn't look very safe to me. Don't you think this is way overboard? It's not like those people are going to follow me all the way to Nigeria and kill me, so why can't I at least be comfortable while I'm here?, everything is starting to feel like a spy movie"

"First, your Dad is broke, you, you've always been broke, houses in Lagos are expensive, you can't live with me because I live with two other men like beasts, so be calm agent Hilal," he chuckled and unlocked the door.

The inside looked better than the outside. The living room looked comfortable with a purple love seat, pink rug and small plasma TV, the room was moderately large; it had a bed, a fridge and a wardrobe. The kitchen was pretty small and the window was small too. It wasn't as bad as I thought it would be.

"Imran, where's the bathroom?" I asked looking around the room.

He picked up his bag, moved his head in a slow motion, smiled, and then said, "You'll find that out on your own. Now I have to go, there are some things I need to do, and places I need to be. Everything's going to be totally fine," He winked and started walking to the door, "take care, I'll see you tomorrow. Fridge is stocked. Bye," he rushed the words out and blew kisses.

I sighed and caught his air kisses, "bye."

I sank on the bed immediately he left, feeling very lonely. I thought about my father, what he was doing and whether he was okay. I performed ablution with water from the fridge, and then prayed. I sprawled on the bed, and fell asleep seconds later with tears strolling down my face.

CHAPTER THREE

HADIZAT

I woke up to voices chattering outside, with sore legs and a slight headache. It was way too early to be so noisy; I just had to wonder if Lagosians never slept. The sun was still hours away from coming out, it was barely five in the morning. I lazily pulled myself up from the bed and went to peep outside the room.

There were queues outside with people holding buckets in their hands and sponges hanged on their shoulders. The men had towels hanging over their necks down to their chests, while the women had wrappers and towels tied above their breasts. I finally concluded that the long queue was leading to the bathroom, or not. I groaned inwardly knowing that the answer was the former.

I was still sleepy but I needed to pray and take a bath, I reeked. I sat down for a while thinking about how I was going to use a public bathroom, I had never shared a bathroom before talk more of a public bathroom. After minutes of contemplating, I decided to sleep for an hour, hoping the queue would be shorter or non-existent by the time I woke up.

I woke up almost exactly an hour later and searched for my bag of toiletries; I found a small bucket in the kitchen and strolled out. The queue was still there, only way shorter, it just looked like the whole neighbourhood showered in those four bathrooms. I walked slowly towards the queue, dreading an introduction in front of a bathroom when I suddenly felt a body collide with mine, making me loose balance and almost fall. I raised my head to look up and saw a girl, or a woman, I couldn't figure it out immediately.

"Good morning," she greeted waving her hand, "and sorry."

"Uhm...uh...it's okay," I stuttered.

I vaguely recognized the voice, then tried to remember where I knew it from, and then it clicked. It was Kenny.

"Kenny?" I asked.

"Deeza?" she asked sounding as surprised as I was, but before I could say anything she was already hugging the life out of me. She hugged me like we were long lost friends who hadn't seen each other in years, while I just stood awkwardly like a sack of potatoes.

"Are you our new neighbour or you just came to shower?" She asked confirming my suspicions. The whole neighbourhood shared bathrooms.

"Yes, I just moved in last night," I pointed at my room, "that room over there."

"Eyyah, I've been wondering who was going to move in there, and I'm glad it's you. Your parents nko or who do you live with?"

"I live alone."

"Alone?" her eyes dilated and looking truly surprised.

I nodded, "I should join the line. I smell of sweat. See you later." I left her and went to join the line, after she promised to come visit.

The bathroom was very different from what I was used to. It was small, with little holes above, it had a pit toilet and the floors were cemented. At the far edge of the bathroom the floor was tiled with a tap and drainage on the floor.

I stood there simply staring for several minutes, until people started banging on the door and speaking in harsh tones. I couldn't do it; I wasn't able to bring myself to actually use the bathroom. I picked up the bucket and stormed out of the bathroom, ignoring the looks I got from people. More than anything, I wanted to close my eyes and be back in America, but I knew that wouldn't happen.

SALIM

My week was being occupied by the deep blue sea and the lion's den. I was involved in two things I didn't want to be doing at that moment. I had sets of dates my dad had personally planned with Fatima and I also had a project at work. At that moment of my life all I wanted to do was take a really long vacation and just take a break from everything, but that was impossible. I wasn't a lazy person, not at all; I was just exhausted after working my butt off in the states for two months.

I lay on the bed with my hands below my head and headphone over my head blasting one of Michael Jackson's songs, when I was interrupted by my father's voice.

"Are you busy today? I would like to set you up for lunch with Fatima at the 'Exquisite', he said dramatically, "it would be nice, so I hope you're not busy today?"

I thought about my answer fast but carefully, and then I said, "You know, actually father, I'm quite busy. I have to go survey the project site with Dayo from the office, so I'm sorry father, maybe next time."

He frowned, "Next time, okay," he said and left the room, defeated.

I called Dayo before my father beat me to it, and asked him to meet me at Obalende.

HADIZAT

Within two weeks, I had realized that I lived among different but wonderful people who had different lives and stories. Kenny and I became good friends, not surprising. I met Wale, his brother Femi and their funny mother who was called Mama Sharp, because she ran a fast food stall called *Sharp*. Wale and Femi, although identical twins had very different personalities. While Wale was calm, a bit quiet, smiled a lot and tried too hard to please everyone, Femi was an extrovert, hot headed and very carefree, he was kind of like the black sheep of the family, according to what Kenny told me. I was closer to Wale and we hanged out more together.

My next door neighbour was anty Samira, who was a very talkative woman and was quite interesting. She had a mental disorder, not too critical though. She had lost her husband and all three children in a car accident three years ago, and ever since, she wasn't the same. Anty Samira would sometimes loose it and start talking alone and sometimes she broke down crying. Other times when she was sober, she was absolutely amazing to be around. I also discovered that the word *'anty'* didn't necessarily mean you were anyone's aunt; it was just what people called female strangers. If they were a lot older, then you call them mummy. For the men, you call them *unku* and daddy, depending on perceived age as earlier stated.

The rest of the people in the compound were all wonderful too, but there were a few grumpy ones too. The people in the compound had nicknamed me 'Anty Ajebo,' I didn't know why or what it meant, and each time I asked Kenny what it meant, she'd simply laugh and not answer my question. Kenny sometimes called me Americanah because of the way I spoke.

I learnt how to shout NEPA whenever the lights went out, which happened often. Wale told me NEPA meant never expect power always and that they had changed the name to PHCN but it wasn't as 'sweet' as NEPA. I got used to the fact there was nothing like peace and quiet in Lagos, except if you lived in the big man's neighbourhood. I learnt the lyrics of popular songs that the barbershops and the cassette shops played every night like 'shake body' and 'shoki'. I thought the dance styles were funny and used up too much energy, but Kenny made them look very easy.

***

Kenny told me she always went to the market every weekend where she sold palm oil. She had asked me to accompany her and I agreed, because I was dying to actually see the market, completely forgetting the palm oil selling part.

I woke up very early in the morning, very excited. I took my bath before everyone else in the complex. I wore a yellow blouse, blue jeans, a mustard coloured veil and wedges. I applied little make up on my face and was checking myself out in the mirror when I heard a knock at the door. Of course, I knew who it was. I flipped the door open and Kenny was outside with an additional company, Wale. Kenny wore a simple long skirt, a sleeveless top and scarf tied on her head, while Wale wore a jersey top and shorts. I looked so off and I knew they thought so too as they stared at me from head to toe with a wide grin on both their faces.

"You didn't tell me there was going to be a party at the market," Kenny said sarcastically.

I wasn't dressed for a party, so I didn't quite understand her joke, but I knew something wasn't right, seeing how they were both dressed differently from the way I was.

"Yes o, I for don ready now," said Wale in Pidgin English. I had started understanding some words in pidgin, but that one was a bit hard to understand.

Kenny said my clothes were too bright, the palm oil would stain it too bad and to lose the wedges if I wanted to come back in one piece.

I quickly changed into a maroon blouse, a flowery long skirt and a black veil. I thought was simpler, but I still got that look from Kenny and Wale that meant I was still overdressed.

***

As I sauntered into the market alongside Kenny, Wale followed behind us, with some of his friends.

"Where are you really from?" she stared at me intensely, "you don't belong here," she waved her hands in the air.

I contemplated in my mind whether it was wise to tell her the truth or not, then I figured she was way too smart to be lied to. She would find out something sooner or later. I didn't tell her everything; there were a few omissions and a few white lies. Meanwhile, I only told her what was necessary to keep her from being suspicious. Even with the very little I told her, she thought it was insane and totally crazy, but she promised to help me in every possible way. We walked all the way to Obalende junction, ignoring the Agberos (touts) that whistled and stared at our behinds,- well I ignored but Kenny eyed them in a way that scared even me, but they just whistled louder and called her 'babe' 'baby' and 'first lady'. When we reached the junction, we met a fight between a police officer and an okada rider. The okada rider was bleeding all over and cursing the police officer who held a blood stained bat and kept reigning curses on the okada rider. People were gathered round them, discussing the fight like they were discussing soccer. Kenny said to hurry up and get a bike man who was willing to go before someone died and a fight erupted, the boys were hesitant to go, but eventually followed us.

The market was called Idumota, located in Lagos Island. Idumota was indeed no place to wear wedges, the ground was rocky and muddy, the roads were congested, with a lot of bumping and pushing. There's literally nothing you won't find in that market. They sold clothes, foodstuffs, fruits, fish, meat, underwear, jewellery, chicken, snails, tortoise, DVDs, hair extensions, everything. There was a section of the market that called juju market where lion eyes, dried cats, frogs, white lizard, skinned frogs and all kinds of creepy things were sold. It had been whispered that if you knew who, you could buy human parts too.

We set the palm oil on a wooden stand with a small shade next to a group of women who also sold palm and groundnut oil. Kenny and I cut and sold fishes all day, while Wale and his friends disappeared into the market. I learnt to stand my ground that day, when people would come and want to bargain on every price you told them, whether it was a cup of oil or a bottle. Some women would try to intimidate you, and others would even call you a thief despite knowing very well that the prices were set.

At the end of the day, one gallon of oil and a few cups in the plastic bucket was left. Kenny said she was going to sell the rest to the retailers in the neighbourhood. She held the gallon and I held the bucket of oil as we chatted with the boys arguing and swearing in front of us. I was laughing at something Kenny had said when I heard a car honk behind me. I was startled, I was about to turn to see what the honk was about, when the bucket on my hand slipped, spilling oil all over the sleek range rover behind me. I ruined the windscreen, there was a small crack on it, and it stained the colour of palm oil.

"Oh my God I am deceased," I gasped. Kenny and Wale just stood looking at me with their mouth wide open, like it was the end of the world.

I went straight to the driver to apologize but he motioned me to the back seat where I assumed the owner of the car was seated. I moved to the back seat, the glass was tinted, but he didn't slide down.

"I'm so sorry; I promise I'll clean it, I'll fix it. Please, I'm so sorry," I begged through the tinted glass. Kenny and Wale also came forward to help me plead with him or her. I couldn't tell since there was still a tinted glass between me and the owner of the car. By then, I knew Lagosians were not very nice when it came to their vehicles, and the owner of the vehicles, no matter how rich or high classed would not hesitate in ripping you to pieces. I was terrified.

We pleaded over and over again, and then kept quiet waiting for a judgement. After about a few seconds, the car door finally opened. I stood face to face with the main character in my dreams for the past two weeks.

"Get in."

CHAPTER FOUR

SALIM

I sat in the car stiffly, watching what was unfolding outside. I was usually never uneasy or nervous about anything. I had barely thought of her since the flight but seeing her again seemed to have had an effect on me.

I thought hard about what to say to her, something that won't give away the fact that I was nervous over a mere woman like her.

I finally opened the door and looked at her sincere, yet very confident face. At that moment I heard myself say, "get in." Why did I ask her to get in? What would I tell her after she gets in? What do I do to her? She stood still; I saw a little look of surprise on her face that quickly vanished. Her friends came forward to try to protest but she stopped them.

"Don't worry, I know him," she said as she got in the car. I looked at her, how could she say that she knew me, just because we had sat on a plane together? She entered the car and I asked the driver to drive. She sat calmly besides me, fiddling with her veil and obviously trying hard not to meet my eyes. She was like a chameleon, one minute she was this confident, almost intimidating woman, and the other minute, a shy school girl. I stared at her intently wondering if she would ever say anything or at least look at me.

"I'm sorry; you can punish me if you want to. I'll pay for it," she faltered a little bit in her speech.

"Could you please stop saying sorry, it's annoying," I almost lost my temper for a second. She kept saying sorry, I wished she would say something other than those particular words. She looked at me for a second, blinked and turned her face away.

"I won't let you go scot-free, but before that, why didn't you call me?"

She looked at me and I felt a bit self-conscious. It seemed as if she was assessing me with her eyes.

She turned her face away and said, "I didn't think there was any need to," I was flustered by her reply, "I had nothing to say to you."

Who on earth did she think she was? She made me give her my complimentary card; only for her to sit beside me and tell me she had nothing to say to me. I stared at her with intense anger and surprise, I didn't know what to do or say to her.

"Uhm, before you stare a hole into my face, can you tell me where you're taking me to," she looked at me waiting for an answer which I didn't have.

We rode in silence and stopped when I saw a restaurant, it was perfect.

"Come out of the car," I said to her, she came out quietly and obediently and followed me into the restaurant.

I found a table and sat down, she followed me, and composed herself in a seat in front of me and simply stared at me, with a look that asked a thousand questions, and said nothing.

HADIZAT

I was about to explode on the inside, I was freaking out and so embarrassed. I've had a crush on the rude guy ever since I met him, praying to see him again. I had finally met him again and I had managed to make a fool out of myself in front of him.

He sat staring at me as I stared back at him trying not to lose composure.

" So," I barely managed to say.

"What would you like to eat?" he asked without taking his eyes off the menu.

How did he expect me to eat in a situation like that? If I had eaten anything at that moment, I would have thrown up and I didn't want to add anything to the list of embarrassing things I had done since I met him.

"'Nothing, I'm not hungry, let's just talk," he ignored me and called on the waitress.

" Bottled water for me and orange juice for her," then he turned back to me, "You like orange juice right?" I nodded. A few minutes later, the waitress came back with the order.

He took a sip and then looked at me, "Drink your juice."

Why was he messing with me? If he was going to shoot me, then why did he have to torture me first? I groaned inwardly.

"My friends are waiting for me; can you please just tell me what I have to do, so I can get going?" I asked with fake confidence.

He opened his mouth as if he was about to snap and reply me, he blinked and then asked, "Where do you stay?".

"Where you picked me." He chuckled and smiled as if I had said something unbelievable and amusing.

"Ok, where do you work?" I thought about what to say for a few seconds.

"I'm a business woman. I sell palm oil at Idumota. Very fine palm oil". Man, I was a good liar, I thought to myself.

He smiled and then he froze, he looked at me.

"You have got to be kidding me. You can't possibly be telling me the truth. You were on a first class plane, you had an American accent, and you told me it was your first time...."

"I lied" I interrupted him, "I won a cooking competition and I was given an all expense week trip abroad, I'm sorry I lied, I never thought there would be any reason for you to find out the truth."

He blinked, his face was emotionless, he smiled and then said, "why would you lie to me, you barely knew me.

"I thought I would never have to see you again, I don't know, I'm sorry".

He looked at me with a look of disgust. I felt so unbelievably embarrassed; I couldn't look him in the face. He stood up, dropped some money on the table and started walking away.

"Where are you going? We haven't finished talking," I stood up to stop him from leaving. He suddenly stopped, "I've always hated liars; I can't even believe I'm sitting at a restaurant with a liar and a palm oil seller. I never want to see or meet anyone like you again. You disgust me so I'm begging you don't ever show your face in front of me again."

I felt a tear fighting hard not to fall. His words burned my heart; it was so embarrassing and hurtful. I watched him as he left in anger, got into his car and drove off. I sat down alone at the restaurant trying to figure out what had just happened. Was he angry because I had lied to him or because I told him I was an oil seller? Whatever it was, it wasn't reason enough for him to say those hurtful words to me.

I sat frozen, replaying his words in my head when I saw his car drive back towards the restaurant. The car stopped but Salim didn't come out. His driver walked up to me and handed me a piece of paper, then left and they drove off again. I looked at the paper;

"Salim

08172662141

meet me here at four pm next Saturday."

SALIM

I couldn't believe it. How could she have lied to me like that? A few hours ago, she was nothing to me and then she had become a girl that lied to me. I was so angry at her even though I knew I shouldn't be.

I wanted to see her again, I had no idea why. Even with the fact that she had lied to me. I should have nothing to do with her, yet I found myself asking the driver to drive back to the restaurant. I had to see her again.

CHAPTER FIVE

HADIZAT

As soon as I got back, I was bombarded with questions from Kenny and Wale. We were seated in a round table in the middle of the compound and almost everyone in the compound was there. I was the topic of the discussion. Everyone wanted to know how I knew someone with such a big car and what punishment was given to me, but all they got were a load of white lies. We talked and laughed all night. Wale kept on making fun of me and the car-oil incident. Everyone went to bed and left Wale, Kenny and I chatting. We talked about dreams, ambitions and life. Kenny wanted to become a world renowned doctor, Wale simply wanted to become filthy rich, and I wanted to be happy.

The next morning, I woke up to voices outside my room, they were talking in loud but unclear tones, and I peeked outside and saw people outside Wale's house. I was sure it was Wale's brother, Femi's handiwork. He was always getting in trouble and this would not be the first time people were gathered in front of their house because of him. This time the number of people gathered were a bit more, he must have done something big, I thought to myself.

I brushed my teeth, dressed and hurriedly went out to see what was going on. I saw Kenny sitting far away from where the crowd were standing, in a corner with her head on her knees and her arms wrapped around her legs, I walked over to her to get the full gist of what was going on. She always had first-hand information on everything happening in the neighbourhood.

"Kenny"

I called her name as I raised her head to see her face. I was taken aback by the tears I saw in her eyes. She was crying, her eyes were red and swollen with her nose running.

"What is wrong? What happened?" I shook her in desperation for an answer.

"Did Bash break up with you? Did you lose anything?"

Neither did she say anything nor did she answer my questions.

"What is wrong with you? Please tell me."

I looked at her and it was obvious she wasn't going to tell me.

"Where is Wale?"

I stood up to go look for him when she held my hand; she looked at me with tears in her eyes. "Wale is........ Wale is not........ Wale"

Then she burst out crying again

"Wale is what?!"

She wasn't going to answer that question either, so I let go of her hands to go look for Wale. It was almost impossible to get through the crowd in front of Wale's house. I had to push through the crowd to see what was going on in front, as I pushed through the crowd i started to see people crying, shaking their heads left to right and hissing.

"What a tragedy? Ah!! Such a nice boy..."

I heard some people say and others were speaking in Yoruba. I felt my heart freeze in my chest and I silently prayed that it wasn't what I was thinking it was. I kept praying as I moved through the crowd. I couldn't believe what I was seeing, I slapped myself several times to snap out of my nightmare if that was what it was. I felt and indescribable pain in my chest, it felt as though time had stopped and everything else had disappeared and all that existed in the moment was me and Wale's corpse lying on the floor in a pool of his own blood.

Wale's mother was lying next to the body, shouting and crying uncontrollably, I fell on the floor and started crying too, my heart was burning to the point the tears on my face felt hot, the women and children in the crowd were soon all crying, and comforting each other. Kenny walked over to where I was crying, hugged me and soon we were both crying uncontrollably.

Nobody knew what had happened to Wale, his mother had woken up in the morning only to discover that Wale wasn't in bed. She wasn't surprised because she knew that he was an early riser. She was peeling the oranges which Wale was supposed to hawk later in the afternoon, when her son's body was brought to her. They all denied knowing anything about it; they claimed they saw the body beside a well on the road to the beach.

Wale was buried immediately according to Islamic traditions. The whole neighbourhood was in grief, he wasn't popular but those who knew him had nothing but good and amazing stories to tell about him. He had a way of making people around him happy. He had a very kind heart and was generous even with the little he had. He was a cheer leader to many people, it was almost impossible to upset him. He was also very strong religiously; you would always find him at the mosque at all prayer times. The day ended with people praying for him and telling stories about his life.

***

A day after Wale's death, I was lying on the bed in my room when Kenny came inside crying.

"Kenny" I said as she immediatelty hugged me. She held me tight and said in a whisper, "It's all my fault"

"What is your fault?"

"Wale"

"Stop talking, you don't know what you're saying," I hugged her tighter. She moved away from my embrace and sat an inch farther from me. She looked at me then turned her face away.

SPECIAL POV
KENNY

It was about 4:00am in the morning, I came out to ease myself, but there was a long line to the toilet and Wale was standing at the end of the line. He told me he had been having a stomach upset, and had been back and forth the toilet all day. No one was going to let us cut in line, so I suggested we go to the bush at the back of the building. We both went to out, but we stayed at different spots. I heard voices when I was in the bush. I heard footsteps and people shouting "thief, thief", then I saw someone run pass by. The crowd came running after him, they didn't know where he had run off to, and so they decided to turn back.

I waited for Wale for a while but he didn't come back so I decided to go look for him. While I was looking for him, I heard his voice screaming, and I ran to where his voice was coming from. The crowd I had seen earlier were beating him up. About fifteen people were gathered around and they were all hitting him. He was shouting and begging them, he kept on saying "Ah no be thief, ejo, ah no be thief (I'm not a thief, please)" but no one was paying any attention to him.

I wanted to run out there and help him but I was afraid they were going to call me his accomplice and beat me up too. I had seen things like that happen a lot in town. Whoever tried to help was always the accomplice. So I stayed behind the bushes like a coward crying and praying. Later on I saw two soldiers coming to where he was being beaten and I thought my prayers had been answered but instead of helping him, they joined they joined the crowd and started hitting him too. He kept crying and begging but they just continued beating and hitting him with their boots.

After about thirty minutes of beating him I stopped hearing Wale's screams.

"He don die (he's dead)" I heard a man say. "Him neva die na faint him faint (he's not dead, he just fainted" another man said. "the boy don die o", they started arguing. The soldiers left as soon as the people started arguing.

'Dat soldier shoe don break the boy bladder (the soldiers shoe has broken the boy's bladder)" he hissed, "this soldiers sef dey too gra gra (these soldiers are too rough)". I felt dizzy, I couldn't cry anymore, my head was spun and then I went blank.

When I woke up neither the crowd nor wale was there, only a pool of blood. I thought, maybe they had taken him to the hospital, maybe he wasn't dead. I ran back home to tell his mother, when I saw Wale's corpse on the floor in the compound surrounded by a different set of people.

I felt that it was my entire fault, if only I hadn't suggested we went out, or if I had just spoken up when he was being beaten, he wouldn't be dead now. I felt guilty, I was a murderer. I couldn't look at his mother's face or even bring myself to tell anybody the truth. What I had done was unforgivable, even if the world was going to forgive me, I didn't think I could ever forgive myself.

CHAPTER SIX

HADIZAT

I felt my heart shrivel in my chest. I looked at Kenny and I wanted to blame her, but I couldn't, I knew I shouldn't. I knew how it felt to lose someone dear to you, and I knew how difficult it must have been for her to confess to me. Wale and Kenny were very close, they were best friends, and she loved him like a brother, as did he.

I held her closer, and she buried her face in my shoulder, and sobbed. I was in no condition to comfort her, I tried to but I broke down and started crying too.

I took in a deep breath, closed my eyes and said, "You have to let his mother know the truth."

She tensed up and her eyes narrowed, "I know, I know she's never going to forgive me, and I wouldn't blame her, I deserve as much hate as I would get in the future." She turned her face away, wiped the tears off her face and stood up.

"Would you come to me, I don't think I can tell her alone."

I sucked in a breath, stood up and held her shoulders with both hands.
"We are going to get through this phase of our lives together; I'll always be here when you need me."

She looked at me in the eye as if trying to see the truth of my words through my eyes, and then she nodded.

"Thank you."

***

Kenny told Wale's mum a day after we talked, and she was neither blamed, cursed nor was she forgiven. Wale's mum had nothing to say, she just kept on crying.

It had been ten days since Wale's death and neither Kenny nor Wale's mum had come out of their rooms; it was like they had shut the world out entirely. The only person who had been keeping me company was Imran. He came every day, even after I had assured him he didn't need to.

"Come on, let's go, you need to stop locking yourself indoors, life goes on," he said as he literally dragged me out of the house.

I groaned and cursed him inwardly for being such a pest.

"Can you at least let me freshen up," I was on pyjamas and no one had to tell me, I knew I reeked. He folded his arms, made his lips into a thin line, he looked like he was thinking hard whether to let me or not. After a prolonged moment, he blurted, "Ok, you have ten minutes, I'll be waiting for you in the car," he turned to leave but turned back, "you don't want to know what I'll do to you if you're not out in ten minutes," then he left, finally.

Ten minutes, yea right. I wasn't the type, who liked to dress up and stare at the mirror all day, but I'm still a girl and girls like to take their time. I came out fifteen minutes later, and met him flirting with a neighbourhood girl. I had to wait for five more minutes before he came to meet me.

"Ten minutes my foot, I could have taken an hour, and you wouldn't even have noticed."

He laughed and started driving. "Where are we going exactly?" I asked.

"We are going to eat, you've not had a decent meal for days now."

It had been so long since anyone cared what I was eating, or if I was eating. Imran was really caring, even though he acted cool and pretended not to.

I smiled and said, "thank you"

"No, no don't get cheesy on me, it's just lunch."

"Ok, Mr Cool," I said, laughing.

He drove to the same restaurant Salim had brought me to. It brought back memories, the harsh words he had said to me, his beautiful face, huge ego....

"Come on, let's go in," he said pulling me out of my trance.

I got down and followed him into the restaurant, "where do we seat?" Imran asked.

"There," I pointed at the same table Salim and I had sat. He led me to the table and pulled out a chair for me to seat.

"Ooh gentleman," I said mockingly.

"I always try to be," he smirked and sat down.

"I'll order for both of us," he said as the waitress came forward.

"Ok, can I use your phone?"

"Ok but why?", he said and turned to the waiter "I'll have this and she'll have this, with a cocktail for me, and orange juice for her" She nodded and left.

"I have to cancel a dat..... meeting," I said.

His lips pulled into mischievous smile, "a date huh."

"Not....a date...it's complicated," I struggled to explain, "I met a guy."

"Hmm, you met a guy?"

"Not that kind of meeting, anyways, I was supposed to meet him tomorrow but I don't think I can.

His smile slipped from his face, "Look I know this past few weeks haven't been easy on you, but you don't have to stop living. No matter what life goes on, until it actually ends. So, you're going to go on that date, or meeting tomorrow, ok." I nodded and smiled.

Imran could be anything he wanted at any time he wanted, a commander, a clown, a flirt, I thought to myself. Just as he finished speaking, our food arrived. As I ate, I thought about that rude, handsome jerk.

SALIM

"Sir, your girlfriend is here to see you," a petite dark maid said as she came into the room.

"What girlfriend?" I asked confused.

"That is what your father told me to tell you." one date only and my father was already calling her my girlfriend, ridiculous, one more date, and he would call her my fiancé.

"I'll be downstairs in a minute," I said to the maid. She turned to leave when Fatima stepped into the room, the maid bowed and left.

"Hello," she said with a big smile on her face revealing her sparkling white teeth.

"What are you doing here without giving me any notice," I asked her as she sat on the couch and crossed her legs.

"Can't a girl pay her boyfriend a visit when she misses him?" she asked stressing the boyfriend part a bit more.

I smirked, "Ah, I see where father got the girlfriend idea from," I picked up my laptop to check my emails. Truth be told, I'd rather work than sit and talk to her for another minute.

"You can't possibly be working while I'm here," she peeked to see what I was doing on the laptop.

"What do you want?" I asked without taking my eyes off the laptop.

"A date."

She wanted a date so she could finally start calling me her fiancé. Hell no, I thought to myself. "No, I'm busy."

She sighed and stood up, "I hate to do this, but you're going to go on a date with me, or I'd be forced to ask your father directly."

"Do as you like," I chuckled. I found it funny that she wanted to report me to my father like we were ten year olds.

She groaned, mumbled something, and then she sat down and glared at me.

"Fine," it was suffocating being in a room alone with her glaring at me, some air wouldn't have hurt at that moment. "This is not a date, ok." She nodded and grinned.

"Where are you taking me to?" she asked as I drove.

"Lunch." I wanted to go the restaurant where I took Hadizat. My thoughts shifted to Hadizat for the hundredth time. I was supposed to meet with her, but she hadn't even called. She had better not stand me up, I thought to myself. Then I thought about what I was going to say to her when I met her, I had no idea. Not only did I think of an oil seller all day, but I was also going on a date, well not technically, with an oil seller. I just didn't understand myself; I barely used to talk to the workers at my house, not to talk less of an oil seller. Workers! An idea suddenly popped into my head at that moment.

"You're taking me to this cheap place," Fatima said interrupting my thoughts.

I scowled at her, "Cheap place or not, you either stay or you leave," I said as I got down from the car, she followed me immediately.

I was about to get in when a body bumped into me, "hey watch it," I said to her.

"Sorry," the familiar voice said, I looked at her and it was Hadizat, she looked at me and I could almost literally see her heart jump out of her chest out of shock. She looked exhausted and sickly, besides her was a well-dressed man with a smirk that seemed plastered to his face.

" Looks like you have a talent of bumping into people and thing," I joked dryly.

"hey," she finally said shifting her gaze from me to Fatima. She didn't wait for a reply before she started the introductions. "Imran, this is Salim, Salim, Imran". Imran held out his hands and said, *"salamu alaykum*, Salim" I hesitated for a second, I felt a burning sensation in me, my heart felt abnormal, it almost felt like jealousy. I shook his hand briefly and pulled my hands away. We stood for a while without saying anything, before Imran coughed, breaking the ice, "and who is this beautiful lady?" he asked smiling at Fatima.

"She's she's...." I struggled for words, but I was interrupted by Fatima, "I'm Fatima, his girlfriend," she said entangling her arms with mine. I wanted to say she was not, but I looked at Hadizat, she obviously didn't care, so I decided not to care about whether she cared or not.

"Don't forget about our meeting tomorrow. Nice meeting you Imran," I said and walked away, and like a fly Fatima followed me waving at Hadizat and he whatever he was, I watched them drive away and jealousy took me again. For an oil seller, she sure was lucky, having me thinking about her and getting to ride around town with that smirk plastered faced guy in a nice car. I thought about her all through lunch with Fatima. I couldn't wait to see her again, I had been surprising myself so much, ever since I had met Hadizat and I couldn't wait for more self-surprises the future had in store for me.

CHAPTER SEVEN

HADIZAT

"Wow those couple looked really in love," Imran said sarcastically as we rode back home. I let out a small huff and rolled my eyes. "He's the guy you were talking about right?" his lips pulled together tighter, I nodded. He didn't say anything after that; instead he focused on the program on the radio as I spaced out thinking. Whether Salim and his girlfriend looked in love or not, they sure did look perfect, they looked like a couple on the cover of a magazine. If I thought I had the slightest chance with him, his perfect girlfriend had just destroyed it. I mean who is an oil seller to compete with a girl like that. I laughed at my thoughts, then I wondered what he would want to say to an oil seller, he was probably just punishing me for lying and for spilling oil and cracking his very EXPENSIVE car.

"What on earth would I wear?" I thought as looked through my wardrobe for the hundredth time. I was really tensed and nervous, I didn't know what I was going to wear, say or do. Whatever! I decided since it wasn't like I was going on a date, it was a casual meeting, so I was just going to wear something casual. I picked up my long flowing gown and wore it, then I applied a little make up, tied my hair into a bun and wore a small dark veil on it.

I was already a few minutes late and traffic was tight and messed up, as usual, and it took longer since the driver stopped to fight with his conductor. I would have called him to tell him I would be running a little late, but I didn't have a phone. I sat restlessly tapping my foot in the danfo praying for the cars to please start moving.

I arrived at the restaurant thirty minutes late and I didn't expect Salim to be happy about it. I saw him seated at our special table. I sucked in a laugh at the thought of having a special table. I took in a deep breath, braced myself and went to meet him.

"Salamu alaykum, sorry I got held up by traffic," I smiled at him, but he didn't smile back, he just glared at me.

"Wa alaykulmul salam, sit," he said and I obeyed.

I sat smiling like an idiot waiting for him to say something. He didn't speak; he just kept his eyes and hands on his phone.

I was becoming impatient, "so," I said tapping my fingers on the table.

"What are you wearing?" he said looking at me eyeball to eyeball.

I blinked then smiled, "is this question really necessary for this dat...uh meeting?"

He scowled at me, "I invited you out here and the least you could have done is wear something... I don't know... nice," he said tapping his hands on the table.

"And what's the most I could have worn?" I glared at him. I was really trying hard to control my temper, things weren't going the way I had planned. I just needed to get things over with.

"Let's start this over again. How are you....and your girlfriend?"

"I'm not here for chit chat," he snapped for a second but relaxed almost immediately. "How's your boyfriend, Imran, or Iman?" he said waving a finger like he was trying to remember. I wanted to simply smile but I ended up laughing out loud. He thought Imran was my boyfriend, still laughing I said, "Imran is....." but he interrupted me, "Is everything a joke to you? He frowned and I tried to explain to him but he stopped me with his hands.

"Forget it, let's just get straight to why I called you here,"

"Ok," I felt my excitement fade away.

"You're a secondary school graduate, right?" I nodded.

"What skills do you have, cooking, driving, anything?"

"I can drive and I did go to culinary school, remember I won the cooking competition. I told you the last time." I went to a Nigerian culinary school for three days, two years before I graduated. My mom had insisted I joined her at the culinary school, "it will be fun, some mother daughter bonding time," she had insisted. I was glad I accepted, it was one of the most beautiful memories I had with my mother. "Why these questions, are you going to offer me a job, eh?" I asked joking.

"Yes," he wasn't joking, he sounded serious.

"Eh, what?" I asked still not sure what he was trying to say.

"You're going to work as my personal home assistant, help, call it whatever you want. Anyways you'll be rendering your services and I'll be paying you." He wrote an amount on a piece of paper and passed it to me. Was this a business transaction or what? I thought to myself. I laughed slightly but noticed he was staring at me, my laugh quickly turned into a cough. He smiled, at least I thought he did but it disappeared immediately. I cancelled the amount he had written and wrote another one, and then I passed it to him. "fine," he said glancing at the piece of paper.

"How soon can you start?"

"Monday" I blurted out.

He stood up, looked at his wristwatch and said, "Ok, this is the address." He gave me another piece of paper, "8 am to 6pm, I do not tolerate lateness, and uh.... Order anything you like, I'll take care of it. I have an appointment now."

"Anything," I asked with my cutest smile on. He let out a huff and smirked.

"Yes, anything, let me have your cell phone number," he said handing me his cell phone. Wow! I felt awkward, I looked at the cell phone and then at him.

"I don't have a cell phone." He looked at me, obviously not surprised, slipped his hands into his pockets and then walked away. That jerk! I wanted to hit him with a chair on the head as he walked away. I bought dinner for everyone I cared about in the compound and put it on his tab.

SALIM

She was something else; I knew the moment she said hi on the plane. My emotions were being put on a roller coaster, one minute I was pissed with her and another minute, she was making me laugh. I had to hide my laughter and smile away from her several times through our meeting. I really could have stayed with her longer, if it wasn't for the darned dinner I had with my father and Fatima. Lately she was everywhere I was, sticking her nose in my business, acting like my girlfriend. She wasn't worth any business deal.

I got home and my father was already preparing for dinner. He was taking the dinner date seriously, like multiple menus, candlelit, everything was just so overboard. He was so busy he didn't even notice me come in.

"Don't you think this is too much, father?" I asked. He turned and moved closer to me with a big smile on his face.

"Ah thanks for not being late," he kept looking around probably making sure everything looked alright, "I heard your girlfriend likes seafood, right?

I struggled not to snap, "she's not my girlfriend, why do you keep calling her that? I watched him as his smile slowly faded.

"Son let's talk," he touched my shoulder as he motioned me to the living room where we both sat.

"Son, I know you, I know what you like and don't. One thing I know for sure is that you don't like being forced into anything, but son," he paused for a second and then continued, "do this for your father, Fatima is a really nice girl and I need this. I met her father the other day and I might finally have a chance of collaborating with marvel team, and you know how huge that would be for the company, for us."

He had so much hope in his eyes; he really wanted me to agree with him. Galaxy was his life and I knew what the collaboration meant to him, it wouldn't hurt anyone if I just hung with her, until she gets tired and dumps me, I thought.

"Ok, fine father, but you know we don't really need them right, we have other great opportunities."

He smiled and got up to hug me, "Thank you son," I sighed and hugged him back.

"Father, I'll just go to the mosque and pray, I'll be back on time," he nodded and left to continue with his preparations.

You do not want to know how dinner went, let's just say nothing compared to my earlier meeting with Hadizat.

HADIZAT

It had been almost two weeks since Wale died, and everyone was still dealing with it in their own way. For me, trying to forget and just move on with life was my way. Wale's mum and brother travelled to their home town, and I guessed they would be away for a while. Kenny had been trying to focus on the happy memories she and Wale had, she had been glued to their photo album, and when she wasn't looking at pictures, she was watching TV shows they used to watch together.

"Can I come in?" I asked as I peeked through the door of Kenny's house. She smiled broadly, "Why do you always ask?" I took that as a reply and entered. I sank on the couch.

"What's up, mummy nko?" I asked her. She got off the bed and went to turn on the TV, "She's in anty Samira's room......you want to watch Jennifer's diary with me? It was our favourite show." By 'our' I knew she meant Wale and her, they used to look forward to watching the show every Sunday.

"Of course," I said awkwardly. She changed the channel and they had just started.

"I know you don't find the show funny but you still have to laugh when I laugh, ok."

"Ok," I replied, and as she asked me to, I watched and faked a laugh whenever she laughed. It was a very long thirty minutes for me.

After the TV show ended we laid on the bed with our backs facing the bed, staring at the ceiling. "I got a job," I said.

"What job?" Kenny asked absent minded.

"A personal assistant, maid or anything but it's personal."

"For who?"

"You remember the guy whom I spilled oil on his car the other day?"

She sat bolt upright and looked at me, "I remember," she said staring at me.

"He gave me the job. I'm working for free the first month"

"Do you need a job or is there another reason why you're taking the job."

"I could use some extra cash and there was just something that pushed me to take the job, really."

"Something, huh," she grinned and played with her eyebrows.

"Hey I know what you're thinking and it's not it."

"Really, what am I thinking?" I wanted to wipe that grin off her face but I was really happy to see her like that.

"Ok," I said standing up to leave, "I have to wake up early, I'm resuming work tomorrow."

"Goodnight," she said laughing.

"Goodnight you too," I said drowsily.

CHAPTER EIGHT

HADIZAT

The next morning, I woke up feeling rather apprehensive. One voice was telling me not to go and the other kept pushing me to go, "It's going to be an adventure," the little voice said. Whatever, I hurriedly jumped out of bed, performed ablution, prayed and carried my bucket to go follow the queue. If it wasn't a sign from God, then I don't know what it was, the line was very short, it was as if everybody planned to sleep in and not wake up early. I bathed, dressed casually, and I hurriedly took my breakfast because I didn't want to be late on my first day at work.

Finding the house was no walk in the park, it was damn stressful. I finally got there few minutes to eight. Thank God for bikes, they could move through traffic easily. I took in a deep breath. "Breath, relax, breath," I repeated silently as I entered the big house, or mansion- mansion suits the building better.

I knocked on the door and a lady welcomed me with a smiling face. She wore a pink and white baggy maid gown and a hat. It looked like the traditional female Korean dresses. I was already thanking God in my heart that I didn't have to wear the uniform since I was Salim's personal help or assistant.

"Good morning," the maid greeted slightly revealing her teeth.

"Morning...I...am," I stuttered, and before I could find the words to say, she opened the door wider to let me in.

"Come with me, Mr Salim already informed us of your coming," I followed her into the mansion. It was a beautiful place, the design was unique, beautiful chandeliers, fine furniture, and fresh flowers in golden pots. There were a lot of paintings but no family pictures. I walked through stairs, stairs and stairs.

"Wait here, I'll let Mr Salim know you're here," she said before walking away into a room, and came out almost immediately. "He'll be out in a minute, sit please," she ushered me to a seat. I waited for five nerve wracking minutes before Salim finally came out. He looked very different in a good way. He wore a grey suit that looked like they were made for him and him alone. I stood up as soon as I saw him, I was really nervous and when I get nervous, I talk a lot, unnecessarily.

"Good morning," I greeted, plastering a smile on my face, revealing way too much teeth. I felt like an idiot.

"At least you're capable of being punctual," he replied.

"Yes I am boss."

"I'm leaving for work and..."

"I can see that"

He glared at me and continued talking, "like I was saying, I'm late."

"Yep," I blurted out, covering my mouth immediately.

He sighed deeply, "can you just let me talk ma'am," he sneered. I nodded and pulled my mouth into a thin line.

"You'll get your uniform from madam Giggs and she'll tell you everything you need to know."

"Boss, did you just say uniform," I asked, hoping I didn't hear what I heard.

"Yes, uniform, like theirs," he said pointing at a maid. He snapped his fingers twice and the maid came forward. "she's my new assistant, take her to madam Giggs and give her everything she needs."

The maid glanced at me and smiled, "Yes sir," then she turned to me, "please come with me." I nodded and followed her and at the same time, Salim walked away briskly.

SALIM

That went well, I thought to myself, as I walked away. Hadizat was pretty interesting, like a story book- a really good one. I never really liked reading, but I wanted to see the end of that story. She was just strange to me, I had met different girls, but none had ever been as captivating as she was. She had multiple personalities, carefree, goofy, confident, clumsy, shy and intimidating. How could one person possess all of these, plus no other girl had ever been able to make my heart feel the way it did, just the sight of her and I literally feel my heart do summersaults.

I was broken off my trance by the vibration of my phone. It was an unknown number, but I figured it may just be a client.

"Salim Abubakar, who's speaking please?" I asked.

"Salim?" a female voice asked nervously.

"Yes," I answered impatiently.

She breathed deeply, "Salim it's I....your...," her voice trembled and she paused for a second.

"It's your mother." I laughed inwardly; I figured it was just a prank call or maybe a wrong number.

"Sorry lady, you've called a wrong number."

"No Salim," her voice hitched as she tried to restrain herself from yelling. "It's your mother," she said breathlessly.

A tremor of weakness shimmered through my bones.

"I need you please, my life is in danger. Please meet me at *Together Café*, four pm. Salim, please."

A moment of silence, fear, and pain passed. I felt a piercing pain surge through my heart after she hung up. I pressed my chest to ease the pain I felt. I felt like I was running out of oxygen, I had to wind down the glass of the car window. "are you okay?" Mark the driver said looking through the mirror. I nodded still trying to catch my breath.

Throughout the day I couldn't concentrate on anything. I had spent twenty two years of my life hating and not giving a damn about her. She abandoned my father and I twenty two years ago, I was only three years old when she left with her so-called love of her life. Father had told me how much he loved her and how he had only wanted to see her happy, but that selfish woman didn't think twice before leaving.

A part of me didn't want to go, that part was scared of the pain, that part hated her so much and never wanted to see her. The other part wanted to know why, wanted to ask her if she ever looked back after leaving.

I was so restless; I knew I had to see her even if it was for the last time. I left work as soon as it was three thirty pm, and drove the thirty minutes' drive to *Together Café*.

The café was crowded; I wasn't so sure it was a good place to meet. I looked around and there was only one table with a woman sitting alone. Although her back was facing me, I was sure she was the one. I took in a deep breath and struggled to keep my heart and overflowing emotions steady, as I walked over to her. She stood up and her eyes glinted as she looked at me.

She looked the same as she looked in the picture, she hadn't changed much. She lost a little weight and had a few wrinkles on her face, other than that everything was the same. She was tall, dark, with beautiful big eyes. She smiled deeply, revealing her almost perfect teeth.

"Son," her voice shook, I sat across her and stared at her as she stared back at me. I wanted to really look at her because it might be the last time, and it seemed she was doing the same.

"Why did you leave?" I demanded, she looked at me sadly, and then lowered her gaze. It was the one thing I had always wanted to know.

"I loved you son, I didn't want to leave you. I tried for three years, I stayed for you, but I wasn't happy. I wanted happiness, and my happiness lied with another man. I'm sorry, I chose my happiness and took away yours."

"You didn't take away my happiness, sorry to disappoint you, but I've always been happy," I managed to say through a thin veil of rage. "Are you happy now?" I asked.

"Yes, I am son," she said clasping both her hands against her chest, "you have two sisters now," she said smiling sadly.

"Why did you want to see me, and what did you mean by your life is in danger."

She moved her hands to touch mine, "You haven't changed much son. You had a big heart then and you still do. You were always so caring and loving. You've grown up to become a very handsome man. Your father did a good job."

I moved my hands away from hers, "I was three. You never knew me," I said, making sure to sound cold.

She nodded and lowered her head, "My husband borrowed money from a very dangerous man, a lot of money. He ran away when he couldn't pay back and now the man is threatening to kill my daughters and I,...and I know he will, if he doesn't get his money back."

"Stop, you called me to ask for money?" I asked her scathingly.

"You were my last choice, I had no other person to turn to, Salim, my son, please," she begged, trying to hold my hands again but stopped when she saw the blistering look on my face.

"Twenty two long years, twenty two years of pain, hate and yearning. For twenty two years I've longed to be in front of you just once," I sighed deeply, "and what do I get? What kind of mother are you?" I stood to leave but she held my hand. I turned slightly and looked at her, "Did you ever regret leaving?"

She looked at me, she became uneasy and weary, she looked down and a tear dropped from her eyes, and then another one, "I'm sorry."

I walked away broken. I had never felt so much pain before in my life. No one on earth could ever hurt me the way she had. I got into the car and released all the pain I felt through my eyes. I cried my heart out until I could cry no more. Men also cry, sometimes it's the only thing you can do to move on. I drove away with the intention of forgetting her forever.

HADIZAT

I sank in the sofa in the washroom listening to the sound of the washing machine, as they mumbled and tumbled. First days were always stressful but I didn't it think it would be as stressful as it was, being a maid was hard work. The workers at the mansion took their jobs way too serious. They all worked diligently with smiles on their faces. Apparently it was one of the rules to always smile.

I stretched and tried to relax some of the stress on the very comfortable sofa. Whoever thought of putting a sofa in the washroom was a very smart person. I closed my eyes for a second and then suddenly I felt clothes being thrown on my body and face, "what the heck," I said sitting bolt upright.

"Wash them," a maid said harshly. I looked at her from toe to head. She was a tall, beautiful and fair lady, with too much make up on. I stood and faced her with as much confidence as I could gather, "I will, as soon as you apologize."

"For?" she asked nonchalantly. I threw my hands up in the air and pointed at the clothes, "It's not ok to just throw dirty clothes on a person like that."

She laughed and folded her hands, "This is your first day, if you want to last another day, shut your mouth and do what I asked you to do." I was really pissed, I wanted to slap the hell out of her. I picked up some of the clothes up from the floor and threw them back at her, "Make me," I dared her.

The moment I threw the clothes on her was the moment madam Giggs decided to show up. "Perfect timing," I mumbled sarcastically.

"What is happening here," she demanded. This fool here thinks she owns the world, I thought to myself.

"Safia what is going on?" madam Giggs asked again. Oh that's her name. Safia started whimpering and transformed into a completely new character, making my face drop in shock.

"Madam Giggs, I don't know what I did to her, I just asked her to help me wash these clothes because I was having a headache but she threw them at me," she lied almost crying.

I opened my mouth in shock and glared at her. "Hadizat, is what she said true?" madam Giggs asked.

"No madam," I answered with no intention of explaining further, it was my word against Safia's. I didn't expect her to just believe me.

"You can go," she dismissed Safia. Safia walked away innocently but turned back to smile and wink at me. The dubious witch.

"Miss Hadizat," she said thickly.

"Yes madam"

"You don't understand how things work around here. I don't know what exactly what happened here so I'm not going to discipline you. This place is like an office, and in the office, there are seniors, and also, juniors. There is a level of respect you have to show to your seniors. You have to take this job seriously, and if you can't, you let us know."

I nodded, "I want this job and I'm going to take it seriously, thank you madam." She smiled and walked away.

It was six already when I finished everything I had to do; I went to the locker room to change. Yes, there was a locker room for all the maids who didn't live in the mansion. Like I said, the job was quite serious.

"Hi," a smallish dark girl said to me as I was packing my stuffs from inside the locker.

"Hey," I smiled at her.

"Tough first day right?"

"You guessed right."

"It will get easier, don't worry."

"I hope so."

"My name is Amira," she said, extending her hands to me. I smiled and shook her hands.

"I'm Hadizat"

"Can I tell my neighbours that I made one friend today?" I asked flippantly with a sheepish grin as I carried my bag in my arm.

"Yes, sure," she smiled, and then I walked away.

I was disappointed I was leaving without seeing Salim. I was told he usually worked from home and whenever he went to the office, he always came back at four pm. I wondered why he hadn't come back yet. Talk about the devil and the devil appears, his car came through the giant gate as I walked out. I expected him to just drive away and ignore me but he stopped and dropped the glass window down.

"Welcome sir," I greeted him smiling. He glanced at me and then picked up a pen and paper and started writing something down. He gave me the paper and said without looking at me, "Get those for me from the store down the road before you leave." He gave me some money and drove away before I could tell him that it was already past my work hours.

I looked at the list and, "cheese rolls, chips, kit kat," what the heck, are you kidding me. I hurriedly dismissed all the weird adjectives I was thinking of classifying him with and went to get the snacks.

I bought the snacks and decided to take them to his room myself, because I was dying to see what his room looked like. I entered the room and saw him praying, even the devil prays. His room was huge with a capital H. It was painted cream and gold. The furniture was mostly gold, everything looked so fragile. There was a large golden chandelier in the room and beautiful glass vases. Outside the golden framed window through the glass was a small fountain. The room was divided into two, one for the furniture's, TV set, and king-size bed that made me miss mine in America. The other part was occupied by a shelf full of trophies, files neatly arranged, and a few paintings. There were two doors obviously leading to the bathroom and closet. Everything looked so neat and organised. Freak.

"When you're done staring, you can keep my stuffs and leave," he said not taking his eyes off the laptop on his lap. I didn't even notice when he finished praying and even got on the laptop.

"You should eat healthy, snacks for dinner is not a good idea," I said as I dropped the bag on the side table.

"And you should talk less, doctor Hadizat," he said mockingly, over stressing the 'doctor' part. I glared at him but didn't say a word. "You're not allowed to glare at your boss," he said scathingly, still not looking at me.

"uhm, uhm," I stuttered, he had a way of making me speechless. I fiddled with my veil as I thought of what to say. "Goodnight boss," I said and left without waiting for a reply which I knew I wouldn't have gotten anyway.

CHAPTER NINE

SALIM

I heard a light yet annoying knock on the door, followed by a greeting. I groggily woke up and checked the time; it was just eight fifteen am. I wasn't supposed to be woken up.

"*sallamu alaikum,* good morning boss," she greeted again. Hadizat who else could it be. I couldn't let her in; I was a mess, after the snack marathon last night I looked like a train wreck.

"Come back in ten minutes," I yelled out and rushed to the bathroom to clean up. Exactly ten minutes later she knocked again, "Come in," I said as I sank on the bed. She came in looking incredibly ridiculous in the maid uniform. I couldn't stop myself, I just had to laugh. She smirked and bowed down, ballet style.

"Good morning boss," she echoed incredulously plastering her big broad signature smile.

"What do you want?"

"What would you like for breakfast?"

"Maybe you could cook me something healthy,"

"Ok, but I'd have to go to the market first"

"No, you don't have to, my father likes to eat healthy, so you can ask the cook for all the ingredients you need."

"Or I could ask her to make something for you"

"Or you could make something yourself," I said, mimicking the same tone she had used.

She groaned, "Ok boss," she muttered something as she walked away.

"Stop," I blurted out and she turned instantly. "Yes," she answered faking a smile. "Uhm, I'd like meatballs and chocolate tea too."

Shocked, her mouth shaped into an O, "All for breakfast?" I nodded and smiled. She glared at me one more time before walking away.

"You're not allowed to glare at your boss," I said sternly.

"Yes boss."

I had to wait hours before breakfast arrived. It was past twelve when she came in smiling with a tray.

"You're going to love this boss. This would probably go down in history as the best breakfast you have ever had," she said with arrogant confidence. "Taste this," she added flippantly, passing me a plate full green stuffs. She smiled and anxiously waited for me to taste it. I hesitantly picked up a spoon and tasted it. Yep, it would go down in history, but not as the best, the worst. It tasted horrible; it tasted like grass with too much salt. I feigned a smile and tried to make the expression on my face look neutral.

"This is amazing," I lied. My father taught me never to tell a woman her food sucked even if it did.

"I told you"

"uhm before you go, I want to let you know of your daily responsibilities towards me," I said putting away the plate.

She nodded, "Ok boss."

"You must always keep this room clean and organised at all times." She kept nodding as I continued; she followed me with every step I took. "Everything on this shelf must be sparkling at all times, understand?" She waved her hands in front of her face indicating that she understood, "and my closet," I walked into the closet and she followed, "you can never touch my clothes except for my ties, they must be arranged accordingly every day. I get confused when they are disorganised. My shoes must be clean and properly arranged too."

"Yes boss, you can count on me," she said confidently. "and you must never wake me up before nine am, no matter what, even if they was a fire and I was..." I was suddenly interrupted by a knock on the door, "come in."

A maid came in, "sir, your girlfriend is here."

"She is not...." before I could complete my sentence I was interrupted again by my so called girlfriend.

"Hey boyfriend," she came in sinking in the sofa. "I missed you so much, you weren't picking my calls, so I decided to surprise you," she smiled and waved her hands, "Surprise!"

Hadizat chuckled from behind me causing Fatima and I to glare at her.

"Uhm, I'll just leave and come back later," she said awkwardly.

"Good, I was just about to ask you to do that," Fatima said.

"You stay, I'm not done with you," I said thickly.

"Uhm okay," Hadizat replied even more awkwardly.

I turned to Fatima, "Fatima can you wait for me in the living room please, I'm kind of busy."

"No I can't," then she turned to Hadizat, "get out," she demanded. Hadizat glanced at me for a second before looking down, not moving an inch.

HADIZAT

I was put in the middle and it felt very uncomfortable. I felt like I was about to get eaten raw, with the way Salim and Fatima were both glaring at me. I was a little surprised that Fatima didn't recognise me, because I remembered every perfect model features of hers.

"How do you think your father would feel about this maid? She'd probably get fired, and you don't want that, do you?" Fatima threatened.

"Do whatever you like," he said pissed off, "and I'm tired of pretending to be in a relationship with you. Let me make it clear to you, it would never work between us."

"Are you breaking up with me?" she stood up and came closer to him, as if daring him to say yes.

He laughed slightly, "We were never together, but since you thought we were, then yes, I'm breaking up with you.'

A breakup, wow! Shocker. I felt like I was watching a soap opera, they both looked intense. Fatima was literally about to tear him to pieces and he was as calm as ever, pretending to be cool. I could see right through him, there was a fire burning in him.

"You're going to regret this," Fatima threatened again as she stormed out.

As soon as she left, his relaxed face turned into a frown as he released his anger. I moved away from him, "I better go before you release all that anger on me," I said as I moved farther.

He chuckled and laughed at me. Weirdo! I walked away from him looking confused. I bumped into someone as I was walking out, it was Amira and it was obvious she was eavesdropping.

"Tell me all about the break up," she said, dragging me to a corner. "Hallelu o, he finally broke up with that winch," she waved her hands up in the air.

"Hey don't use such words," I reprimanded her. "Ok tell me all about it, I couldn't grab the whole gist."

"Ok, ok," I held her shoulder, " I'll tell you later, I'll be back," I said as I escaped.

My head was on fire, I was just in the middle of a very intense break up and I needed some air. I rushed downstairs where a man was sitting reading a newspaper. He looked like he was in his late fifties or early sixties.

"Good day sir, you must be here to see Mr Salim"

"Good day, actually no," he smiled at me and continued reading his newspaper.

"Uhm, okay....what can I do for you sir?"

"Nothing, I live here, I'm his father and you must be new here."

"You're joking, you're his father?" I feigned disbelief.

"I am," he chuckled.

"But you look so young, you could even pass as Mr Salims' brother." He burst into a hearty laughter and I joined him.

"Young lady you are really funny," he said with a smile on his face.

"Thanks sir, and you have a nice sense of humour, I wish everyone around here could be more like you," I commented glaring upstairs, which made him burst into another round of laughter.

"What is your name?"

"Hadizat Farouq."

"Hadizat, can you get me my drugs from the shelf there and water from the fridge?"

"Sure, but you'll have room temperature water, its best for taking drugs. He nodded and smiled as I went to get the drugs.

"What is wrong with the justice in Nigeria?" he complained as he read the newspaper.

"Corruption sir. I don't know about Nigeria, but I know Lagos. The politicians are corrupt, the government is corrupt, the civil servant, traders, danfo driver and okada men, we are all swimming in a big pool of corruption. If you can't stop them, you join them. That is what is happening to justice, but....." I realized I was talking way too much and quickly shut up. I looked at him and he was staring at me smiling.

"Sorry sir, sometimes I talk too much."

"Sometimes?" Salim asked as he suddenly appeared in front of me. His father's gaze shifted from me to him.

"Son"

"Dad, you're back"

"Yes, we rounded up early, uhm, Fatima told me she was coming today, has she come already?" he asked. I felt a cold wind of awkwardness mixed with intensity pass by. I felt nervous even though the question wasn't directed towards me.

"I broke up with her, father."

***

A few weeks passed by and everything was pretty good. I got to know everyone really well. Salim's father and I would usually sit down and talk about politics and life, he'd tell me stories from his past and we'd laugh and talk until I got called by Salim, who calls for the most irrelevant things. He even got me a phone so he could communicate with me whenever he wished. I got to know him more through all our arguments and bickering. Amira and I became really good friends, and Kenny, well she moved on and decided to try and forgive herself, since Wale's mother already forgave her. I even got to speak to my dad through Imran's phone, and he said he was alright and promised that everything would be over soon. Everything was going smoothly, but I had a feeling, it would all soon come to an end.

CHAPTER TEN

HADIZAT

My head was on fire; the pain felt like I was being hit on the head over and over again with a hammer. My eyes were heavy, I struggled to open it, and then I tried to move any part of my body but all to no avail. Slowly, I fell into another slumber after several attempts to get up.

A few minutes later, I was awoken by the buzz of my alarm clock, I was still in pains and my nose was stuffed. I had the flu and that meant a day or two off for me. I wanted to call Salim immediately to inform him, by inform I mean plead with him to give me a day off but I couldn't call him, he'd curse me for waking him up so early in the morning. I got off bed and barely performed ablution and Salat. After Salat I lay on the praying mat and few minutes later, I felt myself slipping into another sleep.

Hours later, I was woken up by a knock on the door; I groggily walked to the door and unlocked it.

"Hey sleeping beauty, no work today?" she asked, letting herself in. "are you feeling sick? She placed her hand on my fore head. I sank on the bed next to her and grabbed a pillow to cuddle with.

"It's just flu, pass me the phone please," I pointed at it behind her.

"Ten missed calls," she said playing with her eyebrows, "trouble," she echoed. I sat bolt upright and yanked the phone off her hands. It was eleven am already and I had ten missed calls from Salim, "I am so fired," I said as my trembling hands dialled his number.

SALIM

It was quite unusual of her, she was always very early, and she was like my alarm clock. Ten am everyday she would walk in with her signature smile and echo a greeting. I had asked the maids and none of them had seen her yet. I found myself impatiently dialling her number over and over again. I was beginning to get worried. What if something had happened to her? What if she was hurt or sick? The thought of her being in danger made me panic.

I had gotten so used to her being around me. I was used to being woken up by her voice every morning, her smile, her humour, her attitude. She was clumsy but liked to do things her way. She did everything wrong and argued about each and every one of them. She was brave and confident and very funny. I loved everything about her. I loved her.

"I love her, I love her," I whispered out loud, shocked. My heartbeat became faster, my head was spinning. The realization that I was in love with Hadizat made my hands tremble and my heart flutter. My heart was indicating that I was in love, but my head was telling me to ignore it.

I picked up my phone and was about to dial her number for the hundredth time, when her call came in. My heart skipped a beat and my hands trembled as I pressed the answer button. I opened my mouth to speak but my voice hitched.

"Good morning boss," she greeted; I imagined her smiling broadly as she greeted.

"Where on earth are you, and why have you not been picking my calls?" I demanded trying to cover my concern with anger.

"Sorry boss, I'm really sick... I can barely move. I tried calling you but the network was very bad," she explained weakly.

"Sick? I'd be right there, you need to go to the hospital, what's your address?"

"No, it's just the flu, I just need to rest and maybe a nice hot chicken soup," she chuckled.

"Ok," I said and hung up. I called the driver, Mark, and asked him to come up to my room.

"Do you know where Hadizat lives?" I asked him.

He thought for a second and replied, "Yes, I have taken her home once, she lives..."

"Ok, buy a fruit basket and hot chicken soup and take it to her house. Stop at the pharmacy and get her some medicines for flu too," I said giving him some money, "and uhm buy her flowers from the flower shop down the road."

He grinned sheepishly, "Yes sir, what kind of flowers should I buy?" he asked.

"Just buy flowers and please hurry," I said impatiently.

I was about to start a project at work and I just wanted to spend the morning with her because I would be getting very busy later in the day. There was going to be some demolitions at Obalende and I had to get started soon, it was going to be some serious work, which meant I would spend less time at home. Even before I started working, I couldn't wait to finish.

HADIZAT

What a jerk, he just hung up on me. He didn't even wish me quick recovery. I quickly did away with all thoughts about him and continued chatting with Kenny about our neighbours, by chatting, I mean gossiping.

"I knew that that demolition stuff was a complete lie," Kenny said when a moment of silence passed.

"What demolition stuff?" I asked curiously.

"Oh, I didn't tell you," she laughed and then continued, "last month, they was a fake notice at the gate asking us to vacate the building, in a month, because it would be demolished today, it was obviously a prank."

"How sure are you, were they notices on other buildings too?"

"Yes but it was all a prank, we tore them all off."

I felt uneasy, "well let's hope it was just a prank." I had seen the things that happened when the authorities came to demolish houses. Chaos and tears.

She laughed, "if it......." she was suddenly interrupted by a knock on the door.

"Kenny, please check who is at the door"

"Ok," she stood up and walked to the door.

"Uhm, good day, I'm looking for Hadizat," a familiar male voice said.

"Come in, she lives here," Kenny said letting him in, it was Mark, Salim' driver.

"Mark, what are you doing here," I asked curiously with a smile on my face.

"Hello to you too. Mr Salim sent me here with these stuffs," he said pointing at a basket with fruits flowers. "He also asked me to bring you these medicines and," he said holding a nylon bag from Mr Biggs. I was guessing it was chicken, I collected it and opened it, and I was right. I was really touched, just a few minutes before Mark came I was calling him a jerk, and then at that moment, I felt he was the sweetest person in the world.

"Mr Salim was really worried about you, hope you're better now?"

I smiled, "Tell him I'm okay..... or I could call him and tell him," I said excitedly, a little bit too excitedly.

I picked up my phone and dialled his number and he picked up immediately.

"What's the matter," he asked.

"Nothing I just wanted to thank you for everything you sent, especially the chicken."

"Yea, don't forget to take your drugs," he said dismissively.

"It's nice to know that you care," I teased him.

"Care?" he said sounding amused, "I just did what I did so you'd get better soon. Who's going to do all the work you left?"

I laughed at his cover up, "By work, you mean organising your ties and polishing your trophies? I know it's a hard job but I'm sure you'll find at least twelve maids out of all the twelve maids in the mansion to do that for you," I said sarcastically.

I heard him laugh through the phone but he quickly covered it up with a light cough, "just get well soon," he said and hung up.

"Jerk," I hissed as I dropped the phone. I could feel Kenny and Mark's eyes on me. "Why are you both looking at me like that?" I asked without looking at them, "nothing o," they both echoed. I laughed and they joined me. Our laughter was suddenly interrupted by loud chattering and banging from outside. My heart thumped and I hoped it wasn't what I was thinking it was. We rushed out immediately. People were gathered outside, some from our complex and others from the neighbourhood. They were some men in construction uniforms, helmets, bulldozers and other machines. The people were arguing with the workers, and some were starting to get violent.

"Wetin dey happen?" Kenny held our neighbour, Mr Dele on the shoulder and questioned him. He began to speak in Yoruba language, but only Kenny could understand him.

"This is bad," Kenny sighed as she turned to us. She became tensed and nervous. She put her hands on her forehead and trembled. "Kenny, what did he say?" I half shouted impatiently.

She bit her lip, "They are going to demolish this place, the notice wasn't a prank."

"What!" I snapped and rubbed my temple, I was panicking because I didn't know what to do. I doubted most of the people had anywhere to go. I may have had somewhere to go, but what about the rest. I started thinking really hard, but my thoughts were just messed up.

"Calm down Hadizat," Mark said to me, "at least you guys need to buy some time to pack up. There is nothing else you guys can do. I'll try to talk to these people, they need to stop fighting and try to find a solution. You should talk to the supervisor for some time," he explained as he walked away into the crowd.

I walked to one of the workers and asked him to direct me to his supervisor. He pointed at a man at a far corner who was making a call. His back was facing me, making it impossible for me to see his face from where I was standing. I moved closer to where he was standing and waited for him to end his call. Just then I realized that his voice sounded exactly like, I looked at him critically from the back, he looked like, I moved closer to see his face properly. I tapped his shoulders and he turned instantly still on the phone.

I couldn't believe my eyes. Salim looked just as shocked as I was, as he ended the call immediately he saw me. My mouth was heavy and the words were stuck on my lips.

"What are you doing here?" he demanded.

"You're not the supervisor, are you?" I asked hoping he would say no, even though I already knew what the answer was.

"You don't live here, do you?" he asked too, I knew he also knew what the answer was. He turned away and cursed beneath his breath. I stood there not really knowing what to do or say next.

"We need a little time to get ready and pack our things and leave. Can you give us just a day please?" I pleaded.

"The notice was placed weeks ago, wasn't that time enough? I can't give one more day. Two hours," he said firmly.

"What about the compensation, we have nowhere to go," I looked directly at his face, but he turned away and stared elsewhere.

"That has nothing to do with us. We are a construction company and we assume the government already settled things with the residents," he turned and looked at me, "and besides you have somewhere to stay.

There is enough room for you at the mansion, you don't have to worry, just pack your things and I'll take you in my car."

This really got to me. I struggled to contain my anger and frustration but I snapped, "I can come and live in your house, but what about all these other people, can they come and live with you too? People are going to be left homeless and you're asking me not to worry. You wouldn't understand because you've never been poor or homeless. How would you understand when you only care about yourself," I realized I was yelling so I kept quiet and tried to calm down. I looked at Salim and his face was as calm as ever, his arms were crossed against his shoulders and he was staring at me intensely with his jaws clenched, I couldn't read his emotions but I was sure he wasn't happy.

"I'm sorry, I spoke out of line. Thanks for your offer but I'll struggle just like everyone else," I said as I walked away from him.

SALIM

I watched her walk away and felt my heart crumble to pieces. I couldn't quite place what exactly had happened. I was extremely shocked to find out she was a resident at the demolition area and I thought I was doing the sensible thing when I told her she could move into the mansion, but she just snapped at me. She didn't just snap at me, she also called me a self-centred person. Deep down I knew she was right; I had never cared about anybody but myself. I didn't care that these people were homeless. I had been living in my own world, where nothing mattered, but at that moment I realized I didn't want to be that kind of person anymore. I wanted to become a man who deserved a woman like Hadizat.

About an hour later, the resident had already packed almost all of their things out. I couldn't do anything but stare at them as they sadly packed their things. Some women were crying, and others were angry, frustrated, and transferring their anger on their little children who were clinging to them, while some others cursed and complained throughout. Two hours later and they were all leaving one after the other.

Hadizat came out with bags and luggage in her hands, alongside a tall dark girl and an older woman. She avoided looking at me as she tried to walk away without talking to me. I rushed to stop her, "Where will you stay?" I asked her.

She shrugged and sighed, "we'll find a place." I looked at the girl and the woman, who were both staring at me with so much sadness in their eyes.

"Ok," I said giving up, "let me at least drop you off"

"No, no" she declined, "we'll manage." I wanted to insist but she looked like she wasn't going to change her mind so I just let it go.

"Ok," I said and then she nodded and walked away. I silently prayed to God for her to be alright.

HADIZAT

I went with Kenny and her mother. They had no one or anywhere to go to. I called Imran first before we left and told him about the situation. He offered to come pick me up to stay at his place, but I lied to him that I was staying with Kenny at her new place, and told him I would call him when I settle down.

"So, where are we going again?" I asked Kenny after walking for a while.

"uhh," she groaned, "the worst place on earth." We walked to Kuramo beach. "we are here," she said feigning excitement. I looked around the beach, shacks and tents surrounded the whole area. There were so many children and women moving around, and a few young girls in skimpy clothing and make up.

"We are going to live in a tent on the beach," I gaped in shock, but I quickly tried to act cool.

"Yea, unfortunately," she sighed. I looked around and I saw that they were all living like it was all normal. Some children were playing with sand, the men and women were chatting in groups, while others were cooking with firewood at a corner. It felt really strange to me, the kind of suffering and pain people go through, the poverty and hunger and then at another side of the world, people spend money like it's nothing. They spend money on the most useless things, forgetting that there are people like this out there. Some have everything but are still not contented and struggle for vain things like power, fame and more money, when just a little of what they have could change a person's life forever. I realized I was those people.

"Hadizat," Kenny called me, pulling me away from my deep thoughts. "yes," I answered turning to face her.

"Let's build the tent"

"Ok, but I don't know anything about building tents." She laughed, "Ok I'll teach you."

It was just amazing even with everything, these people were able to smile and pretend everything was alright. I guessed life made them strong. I wanted to be as strong as they were.

CHAPTER 11

HADIZAT

I tried to fall asleep again after the subh prayers, but I couldn't. The voices of children crying and the shuffling and the footsteps of people wouldn't let me. The mosquitoes wouldn't give me a break, and it was so cold outside. I realized living under the bridge wasn't going to be easy at all. I lay on the mat waiting for the day to get brighter and for Kenny to wake up. I had no plan of going to work. My boss would understand, after all he did demolish my house just a day ago. I got out of the tent and sat on a block besides the tent. The children were still crying, and others had frowns on their faces. They looked weak, hungry and unkempt.

I noticed a child and his mother from afar. The child was seated on the floor, crying next to his mother who was cracking groundnuts, she picked up water from the floor and gave it to him, but he rejected it, and cried louder. She then picked up a groundnut and put it in his hand; he looked at the groundnut in his hand and cried even louder. She hushed him but instead his crying turned into screaming. The woman became angry and shoved the groundnut into the boy's mouth, who spat it out immediately on her face. She got angrier and smacked him on the face, causing him to fall on his back. I think she realized what she had done and picked him up from the floor into her arms and hugged him. I watched them as the child slowly began to fall asleep in the woman's arm and then tears started falling from her eyes. It was so touching that I felt my own tears fall.

I picked up my purse from the tent and went to look for food. I had just enough for some of us, I figured I would be need some more money soon. I was walking to the canteen saw two little boys beating another boy up. I rushed to stop them but someone else got there before me. He was a young boy of probably thirteen to fourteen years old. He pushed away the boys and picked the boy up from the floor. He was reprimanding the boys when suddenly his hand was on his head, he looked dizzy and was about to fall, before I could reach out to him, he was on the floor. The three boys, who were fighting earlier, ran away as soon as he fainted. I ran to him and knelt down, I felt his pulse and he was still breathing. He was wearing loose clothing and there was enough air. He started to open his eyes, "are you okay?" I asked him. He nodded and sat up.

"Wait here," I ran to buy him some water and milk. I ran back as soon as I could but he had already stood up and started leaving.

"Hey, I asked you to wait," I yelled out as I ran to meet him.

He looked surprised and lost for words, "uhmm," he stuttered, "I thought you wouldn't come back, I didn't expect you to come back," his English was fluent and clear, I was surprised.

"Why would I not come back?" I asked as I gave him the water and milk. He did not reply, instead he stared at the milk and then at me. I motioned him to drink; he opened the milk and gulped it immediately. He drank like he hadn't had anything in days.

"You must be hungry?" I asked the obvious. He shrugged, "It's normal, ninety per cent of the kids here are hungry," he said still trying to check if there was any remaining milk in the pack.

"I was about to get some food from the canteen. Join me, I'll buy," I started walking, hoping he would follow me. He looked apprehensive; he stood for seconds probably trying to decide whether to follow me or not. "Come on," I said persuasively. He finally dropped his veil of hesitance and followed me. I bought food for Kenny and her mum, the crying child and his mother, then for me and the boy who I still hadn't asked of his name. He kept thanking me throughout his meal, and I kept telling him it was ok. He ate and left and left half of the food even though it was obvious he was still hungry. I asked him why, and he said he left the rest for his mother. I asked him to finish eating and promised to buy another plate for his mother.

As we walked to buy food for his mother, I decided to get to know more about him. I was attracted to the little boy in a way that I could not explain. I was really curious about his story.

"So, you know you haven't told me your name yet," I said to him.

He smiled broadly, " Salim, Salim Usman," my heart skipped a beat and I felt something warm in my body.

"You know, my boss' name is also Salim, but he is the complete opposite of you.

His eyes glinted, "Really, how so?" he asked curiously.

"Well, he is grumpy, rude and always frowns." We both laughed out loud.

"So tell me, what's your story, how did you and your mum get here?". He suddenly tensed up and the smile on his face disappeared. He dropped his head down and kicked the sand as he walked.

"It's a long story," he said almost whispering, I wanted him to tell me, but I didn't want to force him into telling me, so I just kept quiet and waited for him to choose whether to tell me or not.

"My parents and I moved to Lagos five years ago. My father got a really good job here, and my mother started a very profitable business and I went to one of the best schools in Lagos. Things were going very well until my father fell sick and died. My mother was so traumatised by father's death that she became mentally ill. My relatives took advantage of this and chased my mother and I out of our own house. We lost everything and have been living here for the past two years now, and my mother's condition has become worse. She is now mad," he said the last word in a very low tune. He didn't look at me; he just kept his gaze on the floor.

"I'm really sorry," I said sincerely. I felt sad for him and wished there was something do. I felt he was special and I wanted to help him.

"It's okay, really," he smiled broadly and looked away. We bought the food and gave it to his mother. She was a young and beautiful woman, she had slippers, cans and all sought of things tied to her body. She could barely recognise her own son. I could see the pain and sorrow in her eyes. I couldn't control my tears when I saw her. I gave him some money to take care of lunch and dinner and promised to come by again.

"Where have you been?" Kenny asked with concern. She was seated on the same block I had sat on in the morning.

I sat beside her, and sighed, "long story." She smiled broadly, suddenly excited, holding my hands, "Good news, guess what?"

When Nigerians tell you to guess, they don't really want you to guess, you're just supposed to ask "what?"

"My uncle in Enugu asked us to come live with him until we can settle down, and you can come with us"

I sighed and frowned, and held her hand tighter, "I'm really happy for you guys, but you know I can't come with you."
"Why, does it matter whether you stay in Lagos or Enugu?" I sighed and looked at her but didn't say anything, but I knew that she knew I wouldn't be coming with them.

"So when are you guys going?" She sighed sadly and said, "as soon as my uncle sends us some money."

I hugged her, and she hugged me back. We both knew the words in our silence. I was about to say goodbye to a friend, it was really painful, and had me thinking about how I would be able to leave the life I had started getting used to, back to my old life.

CHAPTER TWELVE

SALIM

I hoped she would come to work. It had been two days and I had Hadizat on my mind, so much and I just felt I had to see her. I woke up very early and waited for her to come. It was about seven thirty am when I heard her voice from outside, and I knew she wouldn't enter my room until it was ten am, and I couldn't wait that long. I jumped off the bed and rushed to open the door. Both girls suddenly stopped talking and looked at me.

"Good morning sir," Amira greeted. "Morning," I replied as I slipped my hands in my pocket awkwardly. She tapped Hadizat on the shoulder and left smiling. I stood watching Hadizat for almost a minute, but she didn't look at me.

"Good morning boss," she faked a smile and tried to act like everything was cool.

"Are you okay?" I asked concerned.

She nodded and smiled, "Where did you move to?"

She coughed and stammered, "uhm....boss, you're up early, are we safe?" she said and ignoring my question.

"Where did you move to?" I repeated.

"Does it really matter? I'll get you breakfast before you leave for work, the usual right?" she sighed and walked away leaving my question unanswered.

She was so stubborn. I really just wanted to know if she was alright. I was going to find out where she lived whether she told me or not.

I left for work quite early and came back as soon as possible because I had something important to do. I got home just when Hadizat was getting ready to leave. Right on time. I watched her from the balcony and waited until she was a few feet away from the mansion, before grabbing my hooded jacket and ran out.

"Should I get the car Oga, are you going out?" Mark asked me when he saw that I was going out. I would have asked Mark to do the job for me, but it is said that if you want something done right, you have to do it yourself.

"No Mark, thanks."

I followed her from afar, she kept walking, I thought she was going to get a motor cycle or something to the bus stop but instead she kept walking and walking. I was really tired and out of breath already, I might sound lazy, but I don't usually walk long distances. She looked pretty ok with walking though. I followed her all the way to the bus stop but she didn't take a bus, she took a motor cycle instead, and I had never been on a motor cycle before. There was always a first time for everything. I stopped a motor cycle and got on it, still hoping not to get caught. It was the most uncomfortable ride ever, I thought I was going to fall off and die, but luckily for me it was a short distance. She stopped at the beach and paid the rider, before walking away. I paid the rider and got off too, I looked around and she was nowhere to be found. It was as if she had magically disappeared. I followed the path she had followed, but they were no traces of her. I wondered why she would come to the beach, it was late and freaking cold. I felt a shiver run through my spine, I held my arms for warmth and searched for her with my eyes.

"Cold right?" I heard Hadizat's voice. Taken aback, I jerked and fell to the ground. She laughed so loudly when I fell to the ground.

"You...." I stuttered feeling very embarrassed.

"That's what you get for stalking a person," she chuckled. I got off the floor and dusted off the sand on my body.

"I wasn't stalking you. Can't a guy come to the beach for some fresh air?" I lied.

"I noticed you were following me right from the house, so I decided to help you exercise a little, it's good for your health, you know," she sighed and walked to the bank of the beach, where she sat. I followed her and sat beside her.

"Why did you come to the beach?" I asked her.

"This is where I live"

I laughed lightly and threw a stone into the water, "so you're a mermaid now? You really are full of surprises."

"I meant over there," she said pointing at the east side of the beach where they were a lot of tents. I always thought it was the fishermen who lived there.

"You live on the beach?" I asked not quite believing her, hoping she was joking.

"Yes, Kenny her mum and I," she sighed and looked at my shocked face, before pulling her lips into a smile. "a lot of homeless people live here too. Life is not as easy as it may seem. There are a lot of people out there who are homeless, hungry, sick and hopeless. There are people in worse conditions than these people living under the bridge, but that's life huh," she smiled again, but it was a smile filled with sadness.

"Yes and I really wish it was different. I have never imagined this kind of suffering existed. All my life I have lived in my own world. I have everything, wealth, health, I have all this money, but it all seems useless now. I haven't been able to help anyone with it," I said realizing just how vain my life had been.

"It's never too late to do something good," she said almost whispering, "life is short, so let's make something good out of it."

We sat there for almost an hour talking about random things, ignoring the cold breeze that was flogging our souls out. It was crazy, how with every word she said, I fell in love with her even more. I could have stayed with her on the beach talking about nothing for longer, but I feared in the end I would have fallen too deep to let go.

HADIZAT

It was one of the most beautiful nights I had had ever since I had come to Lagos. Just sitting there and talking about simple things, and laughing at silly things made me contented. I waited for him for more than ten minutes to get a taxi. He refused to get on a motor cycle, he kept complaining about his hurt back like a child and my mind could not think about how adorable he was. I said goodbye to him and slipped my phone out of my pocket to call Imran. It was pretty late but I just had to speak to him, else I wouldn't have been able to sleep.

His phone rang twice before he picked up. "Hello," he said groggily.

"Imran, it's me Hilal"

"Oh, you finally decided to call," he said in lieu of a greeting.

"Imran, I need to speak to dad as soon as possible, its important"

"Uhm..." he paused, "is everything okay?"

"No, but it will be as soon as I speak to my dad"

"He usually contacts me first with different numbers, but I'll send an email, and see what happens."

I sighed half relieved, "ok thanks. You're the best. Let's meet at the beach tomorrow, two pm.

I had to take permission from Salim to take a break from work for two hours. Luckily he agreed and asked Mark to drop me off on his way on an errand.

"Mark, thanks for the last time, you know you are always welcome at my house," I tried to start a conversation with him as I sat beside him on the passengers' seat.

"It's nothing Hadiza, I did what I had to do," he flashed a smile.

"Mark, how did you start working here.... I mean you seem, uhm... how do I say this"

"Educated," he completed my sentence.

"Uhm, yes, that too"

He smiled, "You're asking as if you don't know this country of ours'. I am a graduate and so are many of the workers in the mansion. You know your friend, Amira, we went to the same university, same year. We graduated a few years ago, but because of circumstances, here we are...... you also don't look like you belong here. You're funny, smart, and pretty."

I smiled shyly, "Everything happens for a reason, and I know that by Gods' grace, everything is going to be okay.

"Yes, thanks," he said with a grin on his face, "what were you going to say before I said educated?" I laughed and he joined me.

"Well, I was going to say charismatic, charming, dashing, you want me to continue?" I asked blinking like a cartoon character.

He laughed loudly, "Yes continue, I wouldn't mind"

We talked and laughed all the way to the beach where Imran was already flirting with a group of girls. I thanked Mark and asked him not to bother waiting for me because I was going to take long.

"Hey beautiful," Imran said flashing me a smile. I scrunched my eyebrows and put my hand on my waist.

"So, you're going to flirt with me too. I'm your cousin, don't forget," I teased him.

"What? I just called you beautiful. You should be celebrating"

I rolled my eyes and sat down on a bench and he followed me and sat beside me.

"Are you alright?" he asked suddenly sounding serious.

I nodded, "yea. So when is my dad going to call?"

"Anytime soon, he.." before he could complete his sentence, his phone rang.

"If this is him, then he must be psychic," he said as he answered the phone, "hello," he said and then passed me the phone some seconds later.

"dad," I inhaled deeply.

"sweetie, how are you doing?"

"I'm fine dad," I said "and you, are you doing well?"

"I'm fine Hilal, but I miss you so much"

I felt a tear fall from my eyes, "I miss you too dad"

"It will be over soon. You'll be able to come back to America very soon. I promise"

"Dad, life is hard. I can't believe it took me so many years to start caring about people, and seeing just how hard life is. I am so glad I came to Nigeria and even though circumstances made you send me here, I'm just really thankful"

"Hilal. I'm so proud of you. You're just like your mother. Really beautiful"

"Thank you Dad"

"You be alright, okay"

"Okay. Stay safe dad"

"I will"

Kenny and her mum were soon to be leaving. . I couldn't stay alone, and I felt relieved of a duty knowing Kenny and her mum were going to be alright. I had to ask Salim if his offer was still open, I was almost positive it was.

"Boss," I called as I entered his room. He was sitting on his bed, with his laptop on his leg.

"You're back already?" he asked, without taking his eyes off his laptop.

"Can we talk?"

"Sure"

"Okay, uh, is your offer still open?"

"What offer?" he asked nonchalantly.

"Can I stay here, until I find a new place?" I spoke in a rushed tone, he closed his laptop and turned to look at me with a shocked expression.

He relaxed immediately, "Yea, yes, you can stay here. Why not? "

"Thanks boss," I smiled and he smiled back at me. I started to leave, but he stopped me.

"What about your friend and her mum?" he asked looking sincere and concerned.

"They are moving to Enugu"

"Okay," he said and smiled again. He looked so beautiful with a smile on his face. I had never seen him smile so brightly. I stared at his smiling face a little longer than I should have. I wanted to walk away, but I felt like my legs were glued to the floor. He should have been crept out by the way I was staring at him, but instead his smile only grew broader.

"You're staring," he said pulling me away from my trance.

"I'm not, I wasn't uh, you have something on your face," I stuttered and lied.

"really?" he asked wiping his face with his hand.

"It's off," I said as I rushed out of the room. I inhaled and exhaled, realizing that I had been holding my breath in the room. Whatever happened to me in that room had only one word to describe it, WEIRD.

SALIM

I couldn't remember the last time I was so excited. Her moving into the mansion was probably the best news I had received since the beginning of the year. Knowing that she would be just a few feet from me at all times, was more than enough for me. I was also concerned about the homeless people there, I had thought about what Hadizat had said about never being too late to do something good, so I decided to do something. I ordered some food items and other basics to be delivered and distributed anonymously at the tents tomorrow.

I took another huge step, I sent some money to my mother and half-sisters to support them. She might not be a good mother, but I wanted to be a good son, brother, and just simply a good person. It felt really good to do something good. After the night at the beach with Hadizat, it felt like I had to be better for myself to ever be good enough for her, like I had to become worthy, and that feeling made me feel more alive than I ever had.

CHAPTER 13

HADIZAT

I hugged Kenny for the hundredth time that day, and then I hugged her mum again. "I'm going to miss you so much," Kenny said holding my hands. A tear fell off my eyes, I didn't want to look at her because I was afraid we would create a crying scene.

"I'll miss you more, you're the best friend in the whole wide world," she smiled and smirked, "I know right."

I pinched her shoulder and we both burst into laughter and tears at the same time. "I'll call you every day, don't get tired, okay," she said hugging me again. "never," I whispered close to her ears. The taxi driver honked for the millionth time again.

"You should go now," I said as I slipped out of her embrace. Kenny entered the back seat, and her mother entered the front, and then the driver started the car.

"Bye Americana," Kenny said wiping her face with a handkerchief.

"Take care, my daughter," Kenny's mum said with tears in her eyes. I waved good bye to them because I couldn't say a word without breaking into tears. I watched the car go until I couldn't see it anymore, and then I knelt down and cried my heart out. I wiped my tears off and was about to leave when I saw a truck of food items arrived.

I watched them work wondering whose handiwork it was, just then I heard a familiar voice from behind me. "Hadizat," startled, I turned and answered.

"Boss, what are you doing here? Was this you?" I asked pointing at the truck.

"What are you saying? I just came to pick you up, I figured you'd have a lot to pack." he explained.

"So you didn't order this men to bring this stuffs here?" I scrunched my eyebrows suspiciously.

"No, I didn't"

"So you wouldn't mind if I asked them if it was you?"

'Knock yourself out"

"Ok, follow me, please," I said as I walked over to the driver and Salim followed me.

"Good morning sir," I greeted him with a smile. The driver looked at me but didn't reply, "Oga good morning," he greeted Salim when he saw him behind me.

"Ah, so he does know you," I said to Salim in an obvious suspicious tone.

"Of course he should, I'm the CEO of a multimillion dollar company, I'm always on business news, and does simply saying good morning indicate that he knows me?"

I glared at him and rolled my eyes at him and turned to talk to the driver. "sir, please who was the person who ordered to deliver and distribute this goods?"

He glanced at Salim for a second, "sorry madam, we are not allowed to disclose such information to just anyone." I let out a small huff, they both thought I was an idiot, "fine" I said and walked away, "thanks for nothing."

"I'm really proud of you, boss"

"So are you ready to go," he said pretending not to have heard what I said.

"No, not yet. I have some things to finish"

"Ok then I'll wait for you"

"You will?" I asked really surprised. "Don't you have somewhere to be, something to do?"

"Nope," he shook his head then slipped his hands into his pocket. I looked at him with an eyebrow raised, trying to figure out what was wrong with him." We don't have all day, don't you have things to finish?" he snapped his finger to make his point.

We went to little Salim's place to check on him. I needed to say goodbye to him. I spotted him from afar, sitting beside his sleeping mother, reading a book.

"There he is," I said to Salim pointing at little Salim, he nodded and followed me. "what you reading there?" I asked little

Salim who still hadn't noticed me. His eyes glinted and a smile formed on his face, the moment he saw me.

"Purple hibiscus, tenth time already"

"Wow, you must love the book"

"Yes, plus it's the only one I have"

I smiled and pinched his cheeks, "how's your mum doing?"

"She's okay. Good morning" he said looking at Salim.

"Morning big guy," he jammed his fist with little Salim's, "how are you doing?"

Little Salim nodded and grinned, "good"

"Let me properly introduce you guys, Salim this is Salim Usman, Salim this is Salim Abubakar, my boss.

"oh", little Salim said, "this is the boss you said is grumpy and always frowns." Salim glared at me and I looked away.

"No, that's not what I said," I lied.

"Uhm, yeah. You said he was my name sake, remember?" I laughed awkwardly and winked at him understand and shut up.

Salim grabbed his shoulder and grinned, 'So she talks about me all the time, right? What else did she say?" little Salim looked at me; I shook my head and winked at him.

"Well she said you were handsome and very understanding too"

"She did?" Salim grinned and looked at me. "Really"

"That's not...... exactly what.... I said" I stuttered, "Let's just change this topic. Let's stroll down to the beach," I said grabbing little Salim's hand.

We were walking to the beach, all three of us, when we passed a bunch of touts who were smoking and drinking. One of them whistled and kept staring at me but didn't say anything. Both guys glared at him fiercely and yelled out, "hey." The guy simply looked away and pretended not to know what was going on.

"Wow, my knights in shining armour. I feel lucky," little Salim laughed, but Salim kept glaring at the guys.

"So, how old are you big guy?" Salim asked little Salim.

"I'm thirteen," he proudly answered.

"Hey," I said crossing my arms, "you told me you were twelve"

"I turned thirteen today"

"Wow," I said excitedly.

"Happy birthday man," Salim said.

"Happy birthday," I said pinching his cheeks, "what birthday present would you like?"

"You don't have to," he said shyly.

"I want to"

He thought for a second and then replied, "Ok, surprise me"

"Okay, challenge accepted. You shall be surprised. Salim and I would go get you a present, while you go get an ice cream at the shop," I said and then nudged Salim's arm.

"uhm, yeah. Here's some cash for the ice cream," Salim said, giving little Salim some money.

"Thank you," he smiled and turned to leave, "hey what's your shoe size?" I asked.

"Thirty nine, I guess I won't be so surprised." Salim chuckled and waved goodbye to little Salim who was already running to the ice cream shop.

I got into Salim's car and then we drove to the mall, talking and laughing throughout the drive there.

"so what would a thirteen year old boy want the most?" I asked Salim once we were inside the mall.

"A play station"

"A play station?" I raised an eyebrow, "really, a play station, he lives in a tent. They is no electricity, talk more of a television."

"You're right. Well, I don't know what else he would want," he said scanning the mall.

"Well you're a boy, you should know"

"I'm a man, not a boy"

"Yes right. Come on let's just go and get the shoe"

"What, you think I'm not man enough?", he asked as he followed me. I ignored him and continued walking.

"Is this shoe cool?" I asked Salim picking up a *nike*.

"It's cool, but this is cooler," he picked up a *supra*. I shook my head in disapproval, "nop, we are taking the *nike*.

"Fine, but I'm pretty sure he'd prefer the supra." I laughed at his silly puppy dog face and walked to the cloth section. Salim picked a shirt and trouser for him, he said the style was trending.

"He likes books right?" Salim asked.

"Yes he does," I answered excitedly, "Let's go" I said almost running to the book section. We scanned the book section, it was hard finding a book to buy.

"You really love that boy, don't you" Salim suddenly asked.

"I've known him for just a short time, but I do love him. You know what I mean?"

"I know exactly what you mean"

I chuckled, "who would have ever thought I would be at a mall shopping for a birthday present with you.

"things have changed."

I felt the air in the room suddenly get hotter. I looked at Salim and he was staring at me. I should have looked away but I couldn't, I just stared back at him. I saw something in his eyes, and it looked like love or it could just have been my imagination. I felt myself melt in his eyes, and in that moment, what I wanted more than anything was for time to freeze so I could look deeper in his eyes.

"You're pretty," he said still looking into my eyes.

"Did you just say I am pretty," I asked ruining the moment.

"What? I think your ears are becoming defective"

I crossed my arms and looked at him with a smirk on my lips, "No, my ears are just fine. You just said I was pretty"

"What do you think of this book?" he asked, handing the book to me, trying to change the topic.

"This is for children of four years and below," I said pretending not to know what he was doing.

"Really," he said looking at the book again, "I think it's cute."

I laughed at him, "he's thirteen, and way more mature and smarter than most thirteen year olds I know. You think he'd enjoy picture reading?"

"Good point," he said and dropped the book back. We ended up picking half of a yellow sun by Chimamanda Adichie and another action novel, only because Salim had insisted. He said that was what kids were into and that I knew nothing about what boys liked. We argued all through the drive back to the beach.

SPECIAL POV\AN OLD WOMAN

I was sitting by the sidewalk begging for alms when I heard a child crying. I looked behind me and a child of about five years had fallen down, and then I saw an older boy run towards him and helped him up. The little boy didn't stop crying, and then the older boy gave him his cup of ice cream and tried to comfort him. Suddenly one of the street men who usually roamed around the beach, looking for trouble, came toward the boys and started asking the older boy what he had done to the child. He probably thought the boy was young boys who had recently been kidnapping children around the neighbourhood. The boy tried to explain what had happened but the man wouldn't listen. Another man came forward and asked what had happened to his son and why he was crying. The street man then accused the boy of trying to kidnap the child by wooing him with an ice cream. Within a few seconds, within a few seconds random people had gathered and were hitting and slapping the young boy. I wasn't the type who interfered in street business, but I knew it would be cruel of me not to say or do anything. I hurried to stop and explain to them that the boy was innocent. I tried to speak to them in Yoruba language, but none of them would listen, they were all busy hitting and beating the boy who was now shouting for help. The boy kept crying and shouting, while they dragged him away and threatened to kill him if he didn't confess. I tried to push through the crowd but suddenly, I felt a very painful blow at the back of my head and everything became dark.

I woke up moments later to see that the boy had already been put in tyres and fuel poured all over his body. He was bleeding all over, crying and begging those heartless strangers. i stood up and ran to stop them but before say a word, he was already on fire screaming at the top of his voice, dumbfounded. Immediately the boy was on fire, the men began to scatter, while a few waited to see him burn. I sat on the sand watching his body become ashes, wishing I could have helped him. I had seen several incidents of people being burnt, but I had never known whether they were innocent or not. I watched this particular incident unfold in front of my very own eyes and I had not been able to do anything about it.

I was watching his body burn in the fire, when I saw a girl and a boy calling out a name, "Salim," they both yelled out. "Salim, Salim," they kept searching and asking people questions. I walked towards them, curious to know if Salim was the name of the boy whose burnt body was lying in between those tyres.

"good afternoon ma," the girl greeted desperately, "please have you seen a young boy of about thirteen years. Dark, short, and he was wearing a blue shirt and shorts. He was supposed to wait for me at the ice cream shop, but I can't find him anywhere. Have you seen him please?"

I felt the tears that have been holding back, break free. I felt truly sorry for both of them. They looked at me desperately waiting for a positive answer which I knew I wouldn't be able to give.

"Madam, have you seen him," the young man asked, looking confused.

"I'm sorry, but your Salim is no more," I said in tears.

"What are you saying? What is she saying?" the girl asked, confused, looking at the young man and then at me.

"Let's go look for him, I don't think this woman knows what she's saying," the young man said and they both turned to leave.

"Wait," I stopped then and explained everything to them, by the time I had finished narrating the incident, the girl was already losing her mind.

"She's lying, Salim she's lying, she said to the young man, "please, tell me you're lying," she said yelling. I looked at her and could only feel sorry for her. I tried to comfort, and reached for her shoulders, but she yanked my hands off. "get away from me," she yelled. She stood up and ran to where the body was burnt, then she grabbed a man who was nearby by his shoulder and asked him what had happened and he told her his own perspective of what had happened. Just then, the police arrived and were asking what had happened, I decided to walk away, because the last thing I wanted to be involved in at that moment was police business, although I knew getting involved with the police would be far better than the guilt I would have to carry with me for the rest of my life.

SALIM

I stood there with my chest clenched in my arms watching Hadizat crying on the floor. Just then I saw some policemen approach her. I walked towards them.

"Is there a problem madam," one of them asked Hadizat. She didn't turn to look at them, nor did she answer the question, she just continued crying.

"A young innocent boy was killed here in that fire," I said to them.

"Ah, jungle justice. What exactly happened," a police man asked.

"We don't know what exactly happened, all we know is that the boy was innocent"

"Any witnesses?"

"Yes that woman," I pointed but the old woman wasn't there anymore, "there was an old woman who claimed she saw everything there just now, but she's gone," I said confused.

"Don't worry sir, we'll investigate and get back to you."

I turned back to Hadizat who was crying loudly close to where Salims' burnt body lay. I had never seen her like that and I didn't know exactly what to do. I walked closer to her and knelt down, not knowing what to do or say, I held her close to me, and she leaned closer and cried harder, her tear drenching my shirtsleeves. I cried with her, for it was so painful. I had only met the boy, but he was a beautiful kind boy and I knew what he meant to her. On our way to the beach, she only talked about how special he was, and how good it would be if he went back to school. She was so excited to give him his birthday present that she literally ran to the ice cream shop. I sat with her crying in my arms, and all I could do was pray for things to get better.

"His mother, who is going to take care of his mother now?" she said sobbing as I drove her home.

"Don't worry about it, she'll be taken to a mental hospital," I assured her.

"Thank you for everything"

"You should stay at the guest room today, you can't stay at the dorm, you'll need some time alone"

'No don't worry about me. I'll be fine at the dorm," she said wiping her face with a handkerchief.

We got home and without saying a word, she got out of the car and walked to the back of the car to pack her things.

'Don't worry about it; I'll have someone take it in." She nodded and started walking away, but her steps faltered and she would have fallen to the floor if I hadn't held her.

"Thanks,"

"Will you be okay?"

"Yes," she said and walked away.

HADIZAT

I walked away from Salim and ran to the dorm. I couldn't bear the pain I felt in my chest and I couldn't stop crying, I doubted I ever would. "Why me," I kept asking myself. Again and again the people I loved kept leaving me, they left and not in a normal way, but in the worst possible ways. I wiped away my tears and entered the room. I was welcomed by Amira's smiling face.

"Hadizat you are.."

"Not now, Amira," I said and walked to the empty bed and buried my face in the pillow and silently cried out my pain.

"Here's your stuff, princess," I felt a load being dropped on my body. I looked up to see that it was Safia, one of the last people I wanted to see at that moment.

"Thanks," I said trying to ignore her, but she wouldn't let it go.

"So you're our new roommate, cool right. It's nice to be in the same room as the master's slut. More favours for us," she laughed and sat on the bed next to me.

"Shut up," I said emphatically.

"What? Don't tell me you are offended. I knew what kind of girl you were the moment I saw you. You are a smart girl, and you don't let an opportunity like that slip away," she laughed again.

I sat bolt upright, "Go to hell," I said and rushed out of the room, and ran to the garden. I buried my face in my knees and cried out to my content; I suddenly felt an arm encircle me and then another arm patting my back. I looked up to see that it was Amira. I buried my in between her neck and her shoulder and cried. She didn't ask me any questions, she just let me cry quietly as she comforted me.

CHAPTER FOURTEEN

SALIM

Two weeks had passed by and things had been quite rough on Hadizat. Although she acted tough and cool, I could see that she was broken inside. She was distant and every time I tried to talk to her, she would shove the issue aside and say she's perfectly okay. I wanted to know that she was really okay. I wanted Hadizat back. I wanted her to smile through her eyes again, and to laugh like she meant it. It might have been too soon to want all that, and I may have been selfish, because at the end her happiness made me happy, but I still wanted it, because in the end I was only a man in love. What was love but blind?

HADIZAT

It was evening when Salim called me to his room. It was supposed to be my resting time, so I was wondering what on earth he would want. Lately he had been like an over-protective older brother. At first it was cute, but then he became a pest in my life, always wanting to, "talk."

"I'm here. Please don't tell me you want to talk," I groaned as I entered the room.

He smirked, "take a seat." I sat on the seat next to me and waited for him to talk.

"I'm working late today, and when I work late, I eat a lot, eating helps me stay awake. So I need you to stay here and help me work. You are going to do some calculations, and also get me whatever I want, whenever I want," he said grinning.

"Are you serious," I glared at him, hoping he was joking.

"Yes I am," he said pulling out his laptop.

"Ok, for how long would I have to stay here"

"Until I finish working." I scowled at him and groaned.

"The devil is back," I mumbled.

"Did you say something?"

"I said, let's start working," I lied.

I watched him work all night and kept going back and forth the kitchen, because he kept ordering for food and snacks. He was consuming far more than I ever imagined one person could consume in one night. I was trying so hard not to snap. By twelve midnight I was already tired, and he looked like he was just getting started. I laid on the couch and pretended to be asleep, so he'd finally wake me up and have the decency to let me go to bed.

"Hadizat can you...." he started speaking and stopped because he realized I was sleeping, at least he thought I was. He stood up from the bed and walked over to the couch where I was sleeping, and then bent down and stared at me. It felt so uncomfortable, I waited for him to wake me up but instead he moved away from me, I opened an eye and saw that he was shutting down his laptop. Ah finally. He quietly dragged an arm sofa and kept in front of me, and then picked up a blanket and covered my body with it. What the heck is he doing? I was freaking out on the inside but I managed to hide it. I held my breath, because I was afraid if I breathed too hard, he might find out I wasn't really sleeping. He sat on the sofa and continued staring at me, like I was a really interesting movie on TV. I felt his hand coming closer to my face, and then he slowly pushed away the veil which was covering half of my face, enabling me to see him without him noticing. It was the most uncomfortable thing ever, I relaxed and waited for him to fall asleep, but I ended up falling asleep first. I woke up in the middle of the night after a bad dream. I sat up remembering whose room I was in. I looked at Salim who had fallen asleep on the arm sofa, he was curled up, he looked calm and relaxed asleep, the moonlight from the window highlighted half part of his beautiful face. His eyelash and nose were long, and his skin looked really smooth, like a woman's.

Watching him sleep reminded me of the first day I had met Salim on the plane. On that day I watched him sleep almost throughout the flight and there I was again watching him sleep.

I picked up another blanket and covered him with it. Then slowly, I slipped under the blanket on the couch again. I had never felt as safe as I felt lying on the couch in his room. At that moment, I realized I had fallen in love with an angel with the devil's smile. I was in love with an amazing man. Impossible love, was what I described my love as.

SALIM

I woke up around eight am. I had over slept; I didn't even wake up for subh prayers. I stretched my arms and stood up and a blanket fell off me, and then I looked to the right and saw Hadizat sleeping on the couch. I had fallen asleep watching her, and I was watching her again, I couldn't help it. There was a sudden knock on the door which woke Hadizat up. She opened an eye and then another one. She looked at me, then smiled, I smiled back at her, suddenly the smile on her face disappeared as the knock on the door continued. She jerked and sat bolt upright.

'This is not a dream," she said shocked. 'Good morning boss," she greeted and awkwardly showed a little teeth. She covered her face with her veil and started walking towards the door to open it. "good morning sir," she greeted my father.

"Morning Hadizat," he answered awkwardly, turning to give me a questioning look. Hadizat quickly left the room and shut the door. "What was that?" my father asked as he sat on the bed.

I smiled, "good morning father," I said as I went into the bathroom to perform ablution. I performed salat and du'a, and then I picked up my laptop and sank on the bed next to my father.

"I saw the way you were looking at her, you have feelings for her," he said almost sadly. I closed the laptop, wiped my face, and sighed deeply, "I think I love her."

The expression on my fathers' face changed, "you think you love her, but you don't. You are merely attracted to her, but that can be fixed. I think it's time to let her go," he said thickly.

"What, let her go?" I said swivelling on the bed to properly face him.

"She's a sweet girl on the outside, but you do not know the real her. Girls from her background are mostly gold diggers, and for Gods' sake she is not even a graduate. Fire her or I will."

I scowled at him, "I will not fire her father, I'm going to do the opposite. I'm going to let her know how I feel," I said through a thin veil of anger.

"Salim," he called as I walked out of the room, banging the door behind me. What was I doing running away from a conversation, I wasn't that kind of person, I thought as I went back to the room to finish what I had started.

"For the first time since I was born, I am experiencing this amazing feeling. For the first time in years, I actually care, I care about her more than I care about myself. I know what life is now, only because of her. Look I know what you think all women are like my mother, but Hadizat is different. She may not be educated, or rich, but she's special and she makes me happy. I am willing to do anything to be with her."

He sighed and glanced at me then looked away, "Even if it means losing everything you have? Would you still want to be with her if you lose everything?"

"By everything, you mean money, status? Then yes. Right now all of that means nothing to me. What have I been able to do with all my money and status? Absolutely nothing. Hadizat makes me want to be a better person and if she accepts me, I'll readily give up everything I have for her."

"I have never seen you talk about anything or anyone like this. I have never seen this side of you before, but I really like it. I want you to know that if you ever fall along the line, I'd be right beside you to lift you up," he said moving closer to me. I embraced him warmly and smiled.

"Thank you father"

"I love you son"

"I love you too"

"I know, now go get your woman," he said tapping my back.

I slipped out of his embrace and ran out of the room to look for my woman. I nervously searched the entire house, looking for Hadizat, asking every single person I saw if they had seen her. I asked Amira and she directed me to the garden downstairs. I ran down stairs, stopping at the living room to pick up an artificial rose. I knew it was cheesy, but at that moment, I felt like the cheesiest man alive.

She was sitting on a bench staring at an empty space with her arms wrapped around her legs. "Hadizat," I called and she stood up from the bench to look at me. She smiled broadly.

"Breakfast right?" she asked.

"Here," I moved closer and gave her the rose. She grinned and raised an eyebrow, "What's this for, are you trying to play a prank on me? Well let..."

"I love you," I said shutting her up.

Her eyes narrowed and her lips formed an O shape, "what did you say?"

"I said I love you. I've loved you from the very first time I saw you, without realizing it. You might be goofy, awkward, clumsy and a bad cook, but I love all those things about you. I don't care about any other thing, all I know right now is that I love you, like I've never loved anyone before," I looked in her eyes deeply and tried to see if I would find an answer in them, but all I could see was shock. She stood there frozen for moments, not saying a word. I was scared she might have had an inner stroke or something.

"Hadizat," I snapped my fingers in front of her.

"Say it again," she said breathlessly.

"What?"

"That you love me"

I laughed, "I love you." She smiled and shut her eyes.

"I love you. You might be rude, insensitive, a bully and sometimes a brat, but I love you just the way you are. I love you." My heart did triple summersaults hearing the words come out of her mouth.

"Say it again,"

She laughed, "I love you Salim," she said shyly.

At that moment, everything else in the world disappeared and she was all I could see, no emotion existed in my heart, except for love. Our moment was suddenly ruined by the sound of clapping from the balcony. We looked up and the maids and my father were all looking down at us and clapping.

"Man, this is embarrassing," Hadizat said covering her face.

"No, it's beautiful," I said looking at her and smiling with a full and content heart.

HADIZAT

It was our first date together and he had dropped a beautiful pale pink dress on my bed and a note that read: happy first date. Be ready at seven. I quickly dressed to meet Mark who had been waiting for me outside, together with all the maids in the house; Mark was to take me to meet Salim, and the rest to give me the most scornful, hateful look they had in them and to whisper insults that I could almost clearly hear.

"You look beautiful," Salim's Father said as I walked down the stairs.

"Thank you, sir"

"I think my son is a lucky man"

I smiled shyly, "I think his lucky too"

He laughed warmly, "go now or you'll be late"

"Ok, bye," I smiled and left.

I tried to make Mark tell me where the secret location was, but he wouldn't budge. We arrived at our special restaurant. It looked different in the night, all sparkly and brightly decorated. As I entered the restaurant, I looked down and they were roses on the floor leading all the way to our special table where my prince charming was standing. There was nobody in the restaurant; the table was decorated with candles and beautiful wine and food. He smiled broadly as I walked to him.

"This is beautiful," I commented.

"I know," he smiled and pulled the chair backwards for me to sit. "you look amazing," he said sitting across me.

"Thanks, you don't look too bad yourself"

He laughed and pulled out a box from his pocket, "open it". "happy first date," he said as I opened the box. Inside the box were the most beautiful earrings I had ever seen, "wow, thank you, they are beautiful, but I didn't know we were doing gifts, I would have gotten something for you"

"Shh," he hushed me, "you're all I need."

I laughed, "You're so cheesy,"

He laughed and said, "I know, I just can't help it, you bring out the cheese in me." I blushed really hard, to an extent my cheeks hurt.

"I'll make it up to you with the most amazing breakfast tomorrow morning"

"Yay," he said obviously faking excitement.

"Hey, it's going to be really good this time"

"Okay I can't wait," he paused for a second, "and please no green stuffs." I laughed and he joined me.

We talked and laughed throughout the night. He told me a lot about his self and his past, including the really embarrassing ones, but I couldn't really tell him the truth about me. I wanted to tell him, but I simply didn't have the guts to tell him, plus I felt it wasn't the right time.

***

It was our one month anniversary and I was in Salim's arms having a romantic argument about an Eddie Murphy movie we had watched together at the cinema, when suddenly Amira came in the room.

"Excuse me. Sorry sir. Hadizat there is someone here to see you." She said and stepped out.

"Honey," I snickered, "I'll be back, this argument is not over," I stood up and smiled at him and he smiled back.

We had started using endearments. Salim had insisted on the second day of our relationship. He ignored me whenever I called him boss and only answered when I used endearments. He calls me sweetheart or baby in front of everyone, which was super embarrassing at first, and it still sounded weird every time I used them, since I had never been in a relationship before.

I stepped out to talk to Amira who was waiting for me outside the room. "what's up, who is here to see me?" I asked her.

"He said his name is Imran and that he is your cousin, he is downstairs sha,"

"Ok thanks," I said, and went to the garden to meet Imran.

"Imran, what are you doing here?" I asked him immediately I saw him.

"Hello to you too cousin"

"I'm sorry, I'm just surprised'"

"Doesn't matter, I have good news for you"

"What is it?"

"Your father won his case, Hilal"

I squeaked excitedly. 'that's amazing"

"Yes, it's over now and you can go back to America,"

"Go back" I said realizing what it meant. It meant going back to my old life. It meant leaving behind everything I had built in Nigeria. Suddenly it didn't feel that amazing anymore.

"You don't seem happy," Imran said looking into my eyes.

"I am happy, I'm just not sure I want to go back to America and leave everything behind"

"I know exactly how you feel, but you're strong sister. You'll be alright no matter what decision you make," his phone rang and he gave it to me. "it's your dad."

"Hello dad"

"Hi sweetie. Imran told you the good news right?"

"Yes, congratulations"

"Thanks, finally we'd be together after such a long time"

"Yes. What's wrong Hilal, you don't seem very happy"

"Of course I'm happy, I just can't wait"

"Okay sweetie, I'll see you in a week"

"Bye dad"

"Bye sweet." I hung up and gave the phone back to Imran.

"Hilal, you have one week to decide." I nodded, I had no idea what I wanted to do. I had a life, a dad and law school in America, on the other hand, I had a life, friends and love in Nigeria. I was so confused.

CHAPTER FIFTEEN

SALIM

I couldn't believe what I had seen and heard. I didn't mean to, but I did, I saw the entire conversation Hadizat or Hilal, had with her cousin from the balcony. I felt terribly hurt, she had lied to me again, and even worse, she was about to leave me. I went back to the room and waited for her, I wanted her to tell the story herself.

She came in a few minutes later, looking normal like nothing had happened.

"Like I was saying," she echoed and sank on the bed next to me.

"You lied to me," I looked in her eyes and saw the pain in them.

"What lie?" she asked confused.

"Hilal," I paused and swallowed hard, "tell me the whole truth." She looked at me and a tear fell from her eyes. She then told me everything, from the beginning to the end.

"Why hadn't you told me earlier. Why did I have to find out the truth like this?" I asked. She stood up and paced around the room, "I was waiting for the right time"

"Right time, huh, they is no such thing as the right time"

"I know that now, I'm sorry," she said sincerely.

"Are you leaving?" I asked breathlessly.

"I don't know"

"What do you mean you don't know," I yelled, "you can't leave me, not after everything," I said standing up to face her.

"I'm sorry Salim, I just don't know"

"Fine, leave, go away and never show your face in front of me again," I yelled and left the room in anger.

I knew that if she left me, I wouldn't survive. I was so scared of losing her, the thought of her not being where I was scared me.

HADIZAT GOES BACK TO BEING HILAL FROM THE NEXT PAGE

HILAL

It had been a week and I hadn't spoken to Salim since our fight. He avoided me throughout and kept the door to his room locked at all times. I was confused and he wasn't helping. It was time for me to leave, and Salim still hadn't come to me. I had an early morning flight, I had to leave by four am. I had asked Imran to come pick me and he was already waiting outside. I wasted time getting ready, hoping Salim would come to see me before I left, but he didn't. I packed my bags and said goodbye to everyone but

Salim. Amira kept crying and hugging me, like more than a hundred times. Salim's dad was really sad to see me leave.

"Are you sure about this?" Salim's dad asked again and again I answered, "I'm not." He smiled and said, "You're a very smart girl, but I hope you know what you're doing. You and Salim are both young, and when we are young, we sometimes make mistakes we end up regretting forever. I hope you're not making a mistake"

I sighed, "I hope so too." I said goodbye to Mark and walked out of the gate, turning back to look at the mansion one more time before entering Imran's car. Imran drove away as I kept watching the mansion, hoping to see Salim run out like in the fairy tales and movie, but fairy tales were just what they were, not real life.

I cried throughout the drive to the airport, while Imran kept trying to comfort me, but gave up when he realized it was futile. We arrived at the airport early, despite all the time I had wasted. I picked up my luggage and Imran picked the other, I sat down and waited while Imran said goodbye to me and left because he had an early morning meeting. Nothing felt right, I felt so terrible. I sighed and buried my face on my lap, when a tear threatened to break free.

"Are you ready to go?" My heart trembled; I wasn't sleeping, so there was no way I was dreaming. I slowly sat upright to see that it was him. He was standing in front of me with his luggage in his hand.

"Salim," I squeaked and went closer to him, to make sure I wasn't seeing things. "It's you...you came," I said stating the obvious.

"I'm just following my heart. You are my heart and I go wherever my heart goes."

My smile grew bigger, "I was going to come back to Nigeria after seeing my dad, I just wanted to know that you wanted me back as much as I wanted to come back"

"Are you kidding me," he said surprised, "wasn't it obvious that I wouldn't survive without you close to me?" he said with his hands on his chest. I grinned and wanted to jump up in excitement.

"God.... I love you so much, my heart hurts. Marry me," I blurted out. He raised an eyebrow and grinned.

"Did you just ask me to marry you?"

I laughed awkwardly, "I think your ears are defective"

"Nope," he said hitting his ear, "my ears are just fine"

"Come on, we'll miss the flight," I said and tried to change the topic.

"Fine, I'll marry you," he yelled out as I walked away from him.

EPILOGUE: SALIM

We came back from America a month later and then Hilal started law school here in Nigeria. She moved out of the mansion, even though I was strongly against it. We often went to America during the holidays to see her dad. I was truly happy and to complete my happiness, I was about to marry the love of my life. The most amazing woman in the world was about to become my wife, what more could I have asked for.

HILAL

After I graduated law school, and started working as part of the legal team at galaxy, Salim and I got married. It was the most beautiful wedding ever to the most beautiful man in the world.

Salim and I created a foundation for homeless and less privileged people. Every Saturday we feed up to a thousand hungry people and occasionally distributed food items and some basic materials to the homeless. Salim also built a free school for less privileged children. My dream came to life every time I saw a smile on the faces of those people.

I have also been working hard alongside some other members to eradicate jungle justice in Lagos and other parts of the country, it's the only thing I can do for innocent little Salim who was killed by jungle justice.

Oh and Kenny, she was the chief bridesmaid at my wedding. She is currently in the University of Lagos studying economics. Amira and Mark are now working at galaxy. My dad and Salim's father became best of friends, both currently at a vacation in Dubai. Those old men never cease to amaze me.

And Lagos, I love Lagos. I love everything that makes it what it is. The chaos completes me, the traffic is something to look forward to, the smell of suya, sweat, the Atlantic, Jollof rice, and fumes together create the Lagos I yearn for every time I leave. Lagos is the city where I found love, found myself, and found life. Lagos makes living feel like living.

I believe now that anything that happens, happens for a reason and that the world is beyond what we think it is, we just have to step out of our own little world, and believe in God, have faith and be strong while stepping out.

ZAINAB KABIR TALATA is a 19-year-old fiction and creative non-fiction writer presently studying Law at Nasarawa State University, Keffi (NSUK). Born in Lagos but raised in Abuja where she still lives, Zainab took interest in writing quite early, and has several writing, including two unpublished novels to her name. She believes that writing is not just a hobby, but also an avenue to express emotions and beliefs without interruptions.

SUMMARY

A Lagos Love Story is love story about Lagos, jungle justice, homelessness and teaches the art of risk taking, through its main characters Hilal and Salim. These two, though living in different worlds, and walking different paths, meet and connect in the most amazing way and change each other's life completely, forever.